"Blake, they wan

The smell of gas grew stronger. They were trapped in the abandoned factory. Fear swamped Christine. This attack had been coordinated with the precision of a military campaign, every contingency planned for.

Blake smiled grimly. "Well, we just won't give them what they want."

Christine pulled herself to her feet and leaned against the wall. Spying a crushed metal two-by-four, she grabbed it and staggered toward Blake. He was obviously fighting against symptoms from the gas but was working on the boarded window. She slid her metal under the plywood and put all her strength into leveraging it. She could feel the wood begin to pull loose.

"That does it, Chris. Keep pulling."

The sound of explosions behind them gave her all the impetus she needed. Together they pulled the plywood off the frame.

"Duck," Blake yelled. A fireball shot through the room, igniting any flammable surface it touched. He threw himself over Christine as they were instantly surrounded by an inferno...

Cate Nolan lives in New York City, but she escapes to the ocean any chance she gets. Once school is done for the day, Cate loves to leave her real life behind and play with the characters in her imagination. She's got that suspense-writer gene that sees danger and a story in everyday occurrences. Cate particularly loves to write stories of faith enabling ordinary people to overcome extraordinary danger.

You can find her at www.catenolanauthor.com.

Books by Cate Nolan

Love Inspired Suspense

Christmas in Hiding
Texas Witness Threat

TEXAS WITNESS THREAT

CATE NOLAN

LOVE INSPIRED SUSPENSE
INSPIRATIONAL ROMANCE

LOVE INSPIRED SUSPENSE

INSPIRATIONAL ROMANCE

ISBN-13: 978-1-335-40498-5

Recycling programs
for this product may
not exist in your area.

Texas Witness Threat

For questions and comments about the quality of this book, please contact us at CustomerService@Harlequin.com.

Love Inspired
22 Adelaide St. West, 40th Floor
Toronto, Ontario M5H 4E3, Canada
www.Harlequin.com

Printed in U.S.A.

For I the Lord thy God will hold thy right hand,
saying unto thee, Fear not; I will help thee.
—Isaiah 41:13

In memory of my husband.
You hold my heart, always and forever.

And to my wonderful editor, Emily Rodmell. My heart is full of love and gratitude for your tremendous patience and belief in me during a very difficult time.

"A man in the wrong cannot stand up against a man in the right who just keeps coming."
An old Texas Ranger saying.

ONE

It was all the weatherman's fault.

Assistant US Attorney Christine Davis shot a disgusted look at the raindrops beginning to spot her new shoes. She distinctly remembered a cheerful voice on this morning's weather report promising hot and sunny. Well, he'd gotten the hot part right.

Her phone sounded an emergency alert just as lightning split the sky ahead. A resounding crash of thunder followed. Try hot, wet and scary.

Her car was still several blocks away, so she scanned the street looking for shelter. This section of Austin was undergoing a renaissance and later would be bustling, but at this hour of the morning, there was nothing but closed shops and construction sites.

Another bolt of lightning set her heart racing. That one was too close, and she didn't like the color of the sky. She needed shelter. Now. The rain intensified, driving against her on gusts of wind. *Hot and sunny. Sure.* Next time the weatherman predicted hot and sunny, she was packing an umbrella and boots.

She had no choice but to take refuge in one of the construction sites. Sparing a mournful glance at her

precious shoes, Christine dashed the last few yards,
ducked under the scaffold and pressed back against the
plywood barrier just as a strong gust sent an empty trash
bin crashing against the wall. Clutching her briefcase
against her chest, she huddled in a corner.

It wasn't the most inviting shelter, but at least she was
out of the storm. The building looked like some kind of
warehouse that was being upgraded, but the only indica-
tion it had been used recently was the graffiti adorning
the walls. *Sami and Dave forever, Luis y Maria para
siempre*. She smiled at the mix of English and Spanish.

The sign warning against trespassing was less
friendly.

Lightning forked the darkening sky, closer this time.
"One, one thousand," she whispered. "Two, one thousand."

Bam!

Way too close for comfort. The worsening storm
confirmed her instincts as hail began to batter the scaffold above her head. Seeking refuge in the empty structure surely couldn't count as trespassing.

The door to the actual building stood slightly ajar,
so she gave a shove and eased inside. Jagged splinters
of wood snagged her stockings, but at least she was dry
and safe from the lightning. She only had to stay until
the storm passed.

Hopefully, this was nothing more than a freak thunderstorm. Okay, a freak thunderstorm with hail. What
were the odds? Austin hadn't had a hailstorm in a couple of years. Figures it had to be today when she had
an important court date. Sporting a drowned muskrat
look wouldn't score her any points with the judge, but

if the storm let up soon enough, she could stop home and change.

She took out her phone to check in with her office. No signal.

A sense of unease stole over her. She was alone in an abandoned building, soaking wet, and now she had no phone service. *Don't panic. Inhale, hold the breath and exhale in a smooth, slow motion.* She tried to follow her counselor's advice. There was no reason to be scared. The storm would pass and she could get on with her day.

Except as she grew accustomed to the sounds of nature, she realized that sounds not related to the storm were coming from deeper in the building. She paused, tilting her head to listen. Apparently, the building wasn't as abandoned as it appeared, and the voices sounded angry. Dangerous? Anxiety gnawed in her belly, testing her vow to remain worry-free.

If she was smart, she'd leave now.

Stop it! Tears welled in her eyes as she fought back the fear. *This is not who I am. I am not this fearful person.*

Unable to stand still, she edged back toward the door and peeked outside. A heavy curtain of rain still obscured everything, and hail covered the street like a layer of snow. She had a choice of thunder and lightning or angry men—men whose fight had nothing to do with her. If she gave in and left now, she'd spend the rest of the day upset for letting fear win. *Please, Lord. Direct my thoughts. Let me trust in You.*

A small, tarp-draped alcove, probably intended as a security booth, was just to her left. She could compromise—play it safe and stand in there instead of out in the open. It was the sensible thing to do.

The voices grew louder, felt closer. Christine ducked beneath the tarp and squeezed herself into the corner. The argument seemed to be escalating, but the voices sounded more muffled in here. She closed her eyes and tried to pray, managing only three words before another sound penetrated her haven.

More thunder? Or a gunshot?

The quick curl of fear in her stomach sided with gunshot.

Thunder, lightning and now guns. She would not panic.

Another shot rang out. Christine huddled into herself. Tears glazed her eyes as she fought back a flood of terror. Her fingers clenched her phone, the plastic case digging into her palm. She should call for help. Except she had no service.

Her legs turned to rubber, and she slid down the wall. No. Not good. She had to get up, get out of here. Forget the storm. Bullets trumped lightning.

But she couldn't move. Her legs felt locked in place as if they belonged to someone else. They wouldn't follow her brain's commands. She tried to shake herself out of it. *Do something. Get help.*

Her thoughts froze as the tarp moved. She could see the imprint of an outstretched hand seconds before the cloth caved and a man stumbled forward. Blood streamed down his youthful face. He lurched toward her, his body thrown off balance by his other arm swinging uselessly at his side. A paper slipped from his fingers and fluttered to the floor, but he seemed oblivious.

Christine knew the moment he spied her crouched in the corner. His eyes were glazing over, but for a brief moment hope sparked in their depths. He reached out as he tried to speak. No words came out, just a garble, but Christine had no problem lip-reading his plea. *Help me.* The message shone in desperation from his blue eyes.

Before she could respond, another shot rang out, and his look of hope morphed into a flicker of sheer terror. The hand that was stretching toward her fell limp, and his body toppled over.

Christine stared in shock.

Seconds before, he'd been trying to speak to her, and now he was dead. *Dead.* The word echoed through her brain even as self-preservation instincts kicked in and sent her scuttling sideways away from the body.

Approaching footsteps galvanized her into action. She jumped up. It would be only seconds before the shooter reached the sagging cloth that now barely covered the opening where the man's lifeless body sprawled.

She glanced around wildly, but there was nowhere safe to hide. Panic hit hard, and she started to shake. Her only option was to try to duck into the next room and hope the gunman didn't sense her movement.

Horror brimmed in her throat as she backed up, keeping her gaze focused on the drop cloth. She didn't dare look down at the man again for fear she'd give in to complete panic.

Step by step she eased back, trying to move quickly but without a sound. She couldn't afford to bump into any construction debris and give herself away. With one final step, she reached back, searching with her hand until she felt the canvas cloth from the second doorway. The footsteps were so very close now. She could hear heavy breathing, knew the shooter was just feet from where she stood.

Holding her breath, she turned, slid her hand along the edge of the cloth and peered into the cavernous room. She let out a silent sigh of relief and stepped into the empty space seconds before she heard the killer's voice. "That'll teach you to cross me."

Christine squeezed her eyes shut as she heard him kick the body over. She was afraid to move, didn't dare look, but in her imagination she could see him checking for vital signs, making sure the man was truly dead.

She didn't think he'd seen her. He'd have said something by now. If she stood absolutely still…

"What's this?"

A different voice. There were two of them? Panic surged again as Christine calculated the new odds. Not that an extra person made much difference if guns were involved.

"Is someone here?"

Too late she noticed the bloody footprints. Terror squeezed her throat, constricting her breathing. Tremors shook her entire body. Had she actually stepped in his blood?

She silently toed off her shoes and ran across the room. She had no idea where she was going, but she knew one thing for sure. Standing still meant death.

Afraid to turn back, she ran, dodging sawhorses and abandoned tools. A noise from behind alerted her seconds before a bullet pinged off a joist above her head. She dove behind a concrete pillar and paused to take stock. If she kept running, she'd just be an easy target. Frantically she assessed the possibilities. Off to her right, behind a cabinet, more tarps hung over what looked like framing for a window.

"Did she see you?"

"I don't know."

"We can't take a chance. Find her."

Terror coursed through Christine at the words. The voice—a slow Texas drawl that should have sounded warm and inviting—sent chills down her spine.

All out of options, Christine stopped trying to plan an escape and just flat out ran for the opening, praying it was actually a window. She ran in zigzags and gasped in relief when the next bullet ricocheted off the wood to her left just as she ducked right.

"There she is."

Another bullet splintered the wood framing the window. Praying with all her might, Christine launched herself at the cloth and burst through the opening.

Rain hit her face like a blessing, but the momentum of her jump sent her skidding across the wet sidewalk. She flung her arms out, desperately trying to find balance, but her torn stockings couldn't gain traction on the slippery concrete, and she landed on her knees.

Tears mixed with the rain on her cheeks as she crawled behind a parked car. The men couldn't be far behind, but would they dare follow her out onto a public street?

Almost in answer, a bullet grazed the car's bumper.

Swallowing a scream, Christine scrambled to her feet. Crouching low, she edged along the car, looking for a new escape route. She had to keep going.

There was a car coming. If she could get across first, she could get away. She tried to gauge the distance and speed of the approaching car, waiting impatiently until she was sure she had the timing right.

Just as she moved to dash across the street, another bullet whizzed past her head. She jerked instinctively, and the motion sent her forward. Off balance, her feet slid again on the slick pavement. Her legs flew out from under her, and she felt the sickening sensation of sliding, like a kid on a water slide, on her hands and knees, directly into the path of an oncoming car.

The upcoming court proceeding had Blake Larsen's nerves on edge as he pulled off the highway and onto the side street. He exhaled and rolled his shoulders, trying to ease tension ground in by worry and compounded by the sudden storm. He'd planned to get to court in time to visit with Sofia's children before the custody hearing, but with the storm turning traffic into a nightmare, it wasn't looking good.

A sudden burst of sunlight through the rain glinted off bumpers, momentarily blinding him. He eased his foot onto the brake as he squinted against the glare, barely making out a woman running into the street.

In what felt like horrifying slow motion, he watched her slip and slide directly into his path.

Instinct kicked in. After a quick glance in his mirror showed no one else on the road, he swung away from the woman. Wheels skidded on wet pavement and the car fishtailed. He hung on, holding the steering wheel steady, as he tried to work into the turn and keep the car from spinning back on her.

Long seconds passed before he could make out her prone figure in his rearview mirror. Knowing he was clear, he gently pumped the brakes, fighting to bring the car back under control.

As soon as he was safely on the side of the road, Blake opened the door and eased out from behind the wheel. His leg ached, but he shrugged off the pain and ran as best he could toward the woman. He was sure he'd missed hitting her, but she lay so still that worry reared its head. He called out, but she didn't reply. When he reached her, he knelt, ignoring the throb in his knee as he searched for any sign of life.

"Ma'am, are you okay? Can you hear me?"

She didn't move, not even to blink, as he talked to her, though he could see her chest moving and she had a pulse. Blake pulled out his phone and called for help.

The rain had slowed to a drizzle, and he didn't want to move her, so he shrugged out of his jacket and laid it over her as he waited for the ambulance to arrive. "Ma'am, you're going to be fine. Help is on the way." He hoped talking might reach her, stir her to consciousness.

She began to wake, appearing anxious and restless as she slowly came back to consciousness. Her eyelashes fluttered several times before her eyes opened. The moment she spied him, terror lit her face, and she tried to scuttle away.

Blake smiled gently, hoping to set her at ease. "Ma'am, I think you should lie still. An ambulance is on its way."

He could see her struggling to comprehend his words until the wail of the approaching ambulance penetrated her brain. She was breathing fast, and he feared she might hyperventilate. "Take a breath. Slowly. You're okay. You're safe."

At the word *safe*, her gaze settled on him with a beseeching look. Her teeth were starting to chatter, but he couldn't be sure if it was from the rain or shock setting in. She still hadn't uttered a word, but from her expression he knew she was panicking.

He reached toward her, and she flinched, confirming his suspicions. He flipped the lapel on the jacket to show her his badge. "You don't need to be afraid. I'm a Texas Ranger."

TWO

Harsh hospital lights aggravated the pounding in her head as Christine struggled to wake up. She knew she was in a hospital but had only a vague memory of the ambulance trip. Had she lost consciousness?

A noise in the hall drew her attention to the tall stranger in the doorway. Fighting back waves of panic, she reached for the call button as he started toward her. She was in a hospital. Surely he wouldn't shoot her here.

A gentle smile crossed his face, and he stopped, raising his hands in surrender. "Ma'am, please don't be frightened. You're safe here."

A memory surfaced amid her confusion, and she clung to the words that had brought relief. *Texas Ranger.* This was the man who'd saved her.

Slowly she drew her hand back from the button and tried to return his smile. "I remember. You saved my life." She swallowed hard as the reality hit her. "Thank you," she whispered.

His smile broadened, and he winked at her. "I consider it a good day anytime I can sideswipe a row of cars rather than plow into a beautiful lady."

"Your car. I'm sorry," she murmured again.

"Just kidding. My car is fine. And you will be, too."

"Why are you here?"

He shrugged. "I didn't hit you, but I found you. I felt responsible to make sure you were okay." He gestured to the chair beside her bed. "May I?"

She started to nod but winced in pain. "Yes."

"Do you recall I told you I'm a Texas Ranger?"

Christine wasn't making the same mistake again, so she kept her head straight and answered. "I do."

"Well, ma'am, I don't want to pry, but when you came around you seemed absolutely terrified. I figured it was my job to stay and find out why."

"I shouldn't have run in front of your car."

"Why did you?"

"I was running from the men." She tried to clear her thoughts and focus on his question. Thinking hurt, but she knew there was something important she needed to tell him. "I don't know who they were."

"But they were chasing you?"

"They were shooting at me." She could see confusion written across his brow. "I'm sorry. I know I'm not making sense." She took a breath and started again. "When the storm started, I ducked into the building across from where I ran into the street. I heard shots." Her voice cracked, and she shivered. "I saw a man get killed. The men who killed him realized I was there, and they shot at me. I was trying to escape from them when I ran in front of your car."

She started to tremble at the memory. "I'm sorry. I don't know why I didn't tell you right away." She shuddered. "There's a dead man in that building."

"Did you call the police?"

She swiped at the tear that had slipped down her face

and eyed him steadily. "When exactly was I supposed to call? When I was running for my life or unconscious in the ambulance?"

He grinned at her sassy reply, and she relaxed a bit. "I had tried to call my office earlier. There was no cell service in the building. So even if I'd taken the time…" She let her voice drop off with the obvious. "Will you call them?"

He nodded. "Is there anything else you can tell me first?"

Christine took him back through her morning step-by-step until she'd given him all she could remember.

"May I have your full name and contact number, ma'am? In case there are any questions."

"Christine Davis." She rattled off her office number and saw his eyebrows rise as he recognized the federal exchange.

"Assistant US Attorney Christine Davis?"

"You know me?" Christine didn't even make an attempt to hide her surprise. People in her position weren't usually widely recognized.

"I've followed some cases. A colleague of mine worked the Ansonia trial."

"Ah." Christine nodded in recognition. The Ansonia murders had been particularly brutal, an entire family killed when they'd walked in on a robbery in their own home. She'd taken great pride in putting the killers behind bars for life. The reminder helped settle her. That was who she was, a crusading prosecutor. Not this woman scared of her own shadow.

The Ranger stood to leave. "I'm sure you're perfectly safe here, but I'll have the hospital post security just the same."

"Thank you, Ranger—?"

"Larsen. Blake Larsen." He took a card from his pocket and set it on the nightstand. "Call if you need anything or if you remember anything else."

Christine mustered a smile. "Thank you, Ranger Larsen, for saving my life."

"The pleasure is all mine, ma'am."

"Christine. Ma'am makes me feel like an old lady."

He smiled. "I'll get back to you, Christine, as soon as I know something more."

She watched him go, and the first peace she'd felt all day wrapped around her heart. She had her own personal Texas Ranger.

"Good news, Ms. Davis," the nurse greeted her several hours later. "The doctor is releasing you. There's no concussion, your knees are only bruised and there's just a mild injury to your shoulder. I have instructions, but he says you're good to go as long as you have someone to pick you up."

Mixed feelings rushed through Christine as the nurse proclaimed her freedom. Now that release was imminent, she wasn't all that anxious to leave the safety of the hospital.

Had they been watching? Had the gunmen seen her taken away in an ambulance, followed her to the hospital? Despite Ranger Larsen's promise of a guard, she couldn't forget the last words she'd heard. *We can't take a chance. Find her.*

For the past few hours she'd jumped at every sound. Each nurse who came through the door set her pulse racing. Every doctor or tech whose shadow passed in the hall caused her heart to skip a beat.

Today's events had brought back all the anxiety she'd been fighting for so long. Her therapist thought her panic attacks were a residual effect of her mother's murder when she was young. A mistaken-identity kidnapping attempt related to one of her cases a few years ago had been the trigger. Suddenly no place had felt safe.

The shooting this morning magnified her reaction. Knowing there was a valid reason didn't change her feelings, didn't stop the emotional response. It didn't calm her shattered nerves. She couldn't go through this again. She couldn't give in to the panic.

Taking a deep breath, she pushed aside the dark thoughts in order to deal with the more immediate issue. "I can get myself home."

The nurse chuckled. "Honey, you're not driving anywhere with the meds they gave you."

"Can I call a cab?"

"It would be better to call a friend."

Christine sighed and fought back tears. How had her life become such a mess that she was this panicked person who didn't even have a friend to call?

She slumped back against the pillow. All the years of working hard had yielded plenty of colleagues, plenty of casual acquaintances, but no one she could really call a close friend.

She must have been quiet too long because the nurse spoke again. "Sorry, those are hospital rules. You've been medicated. You need a responsible adult to accompany you."

Christine relaxed. Responsible adult. That she had covered. "I'll call my assistant."

"Okay." The woman nodded and made a notation on her computer. "Buzz me when they get here."

Christine waited until the nurse headed down the hall. She picked up her phone but opted to text, instead. She wasn't sure she could keep the tears out of her voice if she had to actually speak to Sally. Pity was one thing she didn't want.

The pain meds kicked in, and she was dozing when a knock at the door startled her awake. Instinct made her huddle in the corner of the bed. Her gaze darted around the room as she searched for better cover.

"Hello, Christine."

Christine knew that voice. "Henry?" She blinked her eyes in confusion at the sight of her boss. "Why are you here? I asked Sally to come."

"I told her I needed to check on you myself."

His words caused a sick feeling in Christine's stomach. She understood Henry's need to check on her. He had been her guardian, after all. But now he was her boss, and she had fought hard to prove herself to him. She prided herself on professionalism, on her ability to handle whatever life threw at her, so she didn't like Henry seeing her in a vulnerable position. "I'm fine. I just need to get out of here and go home."

"I saw the doctor on the way in. He told me your collarbone is bruised. Melinda suggested I bring you back to the house so she can care for you."

"Doesn't it violate my HIPAA rights for him to talk to you?"

Henry shrugged off her concern. "I explained I'm your closest relation. You've been under stress. I had to understand what was best for you."

Christine wasn't really surprised. The main reason Henry excelled at his job was because he was persuasive. And technically he was her closest relation—legal, if not blood. He'd taken her in when her mother was murdered, and he and his wife had raised her. He was much more than her boss, but that didn't mean she wanted to leave with him.

She just wanted to go home. Alone. Where she'd be safe.

But maybe alone wasn't safe. Maybe she should stay with Henry and Melinda. She fought back tears. Why was she so indecisive? She was stronger than this. She would not cower in fear.

That brought the bigger concern to her mind. "Henry, it wasn't just an accident. I need to explain. I hope the Ranger called the police."

"That's the other reason I came, Christine."

Something in his voice set her nerves even more on edge. She gripped the bedsheets, forcing herself not to pull them over her head. "What?"

"I'm giving you a leave of absence. You can take time to recover and work with the counselor."

As much as he angered her with his assumptions, she couldn't let him see that. She had to stay cool, professional. "I'm fine, Henry. I have a few scrapes, an injured shoulder, as the doctor told you. Nothing about my injuries will prevent me from returning to work after the weekend. I can't just take time off. I've got cases, people counting on me."

"No one's indispensable, Christine. We'll have someone cover your cases. We'll fill in with one of the younger staff members."

She tried to protest, but he spoke over her.

"Christine. You're like a daughter to me. I would be neglectful as both a boss and a guardian if I didn't make you take time to heal fully. And I don't mean this." He gestured toward her arm. "I wanted you to take time after the kidnapping, but you refused. You said you needed to work, so I let you. I was wrong. I should have made you take time off and get real help."

"I didn't want time. I wanted to work. And you're no longer my guardian. I'm an adult who can make decisions for myself." She couldn't believe he was doing this. For years she'd worked toward being the kind of crusading prosecutor her mother had been. She didn't know any life other than the law.

Why was an injured shoulder making him decide she needed to take leave? Even through her painkiller haze, something felt wrong. Henry wasn't one to overreact.

She tested him. "What if I take a week to let the arm heal? Will that satisfy you?"

"No."

His blunt response shocked her. "What's this really about, Henry?"

He looked around, walked over to peek outside the cubicle before pulling the curtain fully closed. He came and stood by the side of her bed.

"The police went to the building. There was no body, Christine. No sign of anyone hurt." He shook his head. "No sign of anything at all."

Not fit for duty.

The words still burned, and they echoed in his head as Blake fired off ten shots in quick succession, each hitting dead center on the target.

The Rangers had determined he needed time to recover physically and mentally from his last case. He agreed about the physical recovery, but aside from a stiff knee he was ready to work. As for the mental, if they expected him to get over losing a woman he was sworn to protect, then no amount of leave was going to qualify him for duty. No matter how many times his superiors told him Sofia's death was not his fault, he still felt responsible.

He checked his stance and fired off another round. There was nothing wrong with his aim, but his concentration was way off.

He was a Texas Ranger and should have been able to compartmentalize, to put this morning's events out of his mind while he focused on the upcoming meeting. It was his Ranger instinct, though, honed by years in the field, that screamed foul about this morning.

Christine Davis had appeared every bit the terrified victim when she'd told her story. He'd had no reason to suspect anything until her version didn't hold up—until no body had been found.

His phone buzzed. He glanced at the screen, then looked over to where his boss was waiting. The man gestured with his head that Blake should meet him inside.

Blake holstered his SIG and left the range. He shed his protective gear and headed upstairs.

"Impressive work out there."

"Thank you, sir. I'm fit. And more than ready to get back to work." He couldn't take another day of hanging around the ranch. A Ranger needed to be active in order to stay alert and at the top of his game.

"What happened this morning?"

So he wasn't the only one thinking about it. Blake debated how to answer. Nothing about this experience was going to help his career, but he had to be truthful.

"The woman said she'd been running from men who were shooting at her."

"That's why she ran in front of your car?"

"Supposedly."

Blake knew the obvious follow-up question. Rather than wait for it, he continued. "She said they'd killed someone. That his body was still in the building."

"But there was no body?"

"Correct."

"And this is a problem for you because?"

Blake swallowed hard before diving in. He still wasn't sure he believed what he was about to do. But he did believe her.

"Thing is, sir, I think she's telling the truth."

The look on his boss's face told Blake he had probably just flunked the mental readiness part of his interview.

Ranger Harris turned and leaned on the railing overlooking the front parking lot. Blake followed, wondering how he was going to possibly explain what seemed inexplicable.

"Let me be sure I have this straight, Larsen. The police searched the building but found no body."

He paused, and Blake nodded.

"But you're willing to stake your reputation on the belief she's telling the truth?"

Blake wished he was still on the range and could fire a few more shots into a target. Because, put that way, it did seem more than a little surprising that he believed the woman—a woman he'd never seen before this morning.

Blake rolled his finger along the edge of his hat, weighing his words before he spoke. "It's gut instinct,

Ranger instinct. If you'd seen the look on her face, the absolute terror, with all due respect, sir, I think you'd believe her, too."

Harris nodded thoughtfully. "I can believe she was scared if someone was shooting at her." He steepled his hands under his chin and slowly tapped the pointer fingers together as he often did when thinking. Blake waited.

"Are you sure she's innocent? Appearances could be deceptive. Maybe she was involved with them. Maybe it was a deal gone wrong, and she's trying to play you."

Blake rolled the idea around in his head, but it didn't fit. "She's an assistant US attorney with a sterling reputation."

"And even her own boss doesn't believe her."

The quick comeback gave him pause. This was news. Why didn't her boss believe her? "You spoke to him? What did he say?"

"That she was stressed from several incidents and probably imagined it. He's insisting she take a leave of absence."

Blake studied the man he'd known all his life—his boss, his father's friend, the best Texas Ranger he knew, including his dad. He knew Harris as a man of integrity, one who would consider all angles and reflect before making a decision.

"Doesn't it bother you that someone who knows her would dismiss her concerns that easily?"

"That's what I'm asking you," Harris replied.

Blake turned and rested back against the railing. He could see the back of the Texas star, high above the building's entrance. That star stood for honor, integrity. He had sworn loyalty under that star, and his vow drove him now. "Should that make me suspect her? Or her boss?"

Raised eyebrows were the only response he got, so he pushed on. "Something happened in that building this morning. Something that made her run in front of my car. So, yeah, the fact that her boss dismisses her so easily concerns me more than there not being a body."

"I never knew you to be taken in by a pretty face, Larsen."

The comment wasn't accusatory but was meant to make him consider. Was that it? Had he fallen for her beauty and vulnerability? His superior was wrong about one thing, though. It wasn't the first time he'd been taken in by a need to protect a lovely, helpless woman.

The last one ended up dead.

Harris eased back from the rail and straightened to his full height. "I've never worked with Assistant US Attorney Davis, but you're right. Something stinks. Her reputation is better than this." Harris put his hat back on and eyed Blake somberly. "I have this problem, Ranger Larsen. I'm afraid I don't find you fit for active duty yet."

Blake's heart started to sink, but something about the twinkle in the Ranger's eye stopped it from free-falling.

"What I can do is assign you to keep a watch over Ms. Davis. Get to know her if you like, see what you can find out." He cleared his throat and walked toward the far corner, beckoning Blake to follow. "Thing is, we know something went down in that warehouse. At the very least, there is an allegation of murder. Since the police aren't interested, and neither is the US Attorney's Office, I'm claiming jurisdiction. As Rangers, it's our duty to investigate corruption. Hopefully, that's not what we've got here because there are some pretty big names involved. Discretion is key. I'm placing my trust in you to ferret out the truth."

The unspoken "don't let me down" hung heavily between them. Blake extended his hand. "Thank you, sir."

Harris took his hand in a firm shake. "I'm heading downstairs. Plan to burn off some frustration on the range. You don't need to hang around. Just keep me updated."

Blake didn't need to be told twice. He grabbed his gear and headed out, but drew up short as he reached the parking lot. Now what? He couldn't just drive over to Christine's house and say, "Hey, I think we should hang out together." He needed a plan.

Ranger Harris was putting a truckload of confidence in him, and Blake knew his boss wasn't just offering him a way to stay busy while on leave. His last case had gone horribly wrong, and a woman had died. Although an internal investigation had completely cleared him of any wrongdoing, Blake still blamed himself for not being able to prevent Sofia's death.

He stared back up at that Texas Lone Star, feeling the weight of the trust placed in him, and made a vow. He would figure out what had really happened at the warehouse, and he would keep Christine Davis safe while doing it.

THREE

A knock on the bedroom door startled Christine awake, leaving her disoriented and confused. Staring around the dimly lit but familiar bedroom, she felt like a teenager again. She rubbed her eyes and tried to remember why she had stayed at Henry and Melinda's house.

Melinda's voice sounded through the door. "Chris, breakfast is ready. Come on down when you're ready, so we can make plans for the day."

Christine rolled over to look at the clock, and memories of the previous day rushed in on a wave of pain. She eased off her injured shoulder and sat up, swinging her legs over the side and waiting for the dizziness to pass. Her thoughts slowly cleared. Henry had brought her here from the hospital, and Melinda had set her up in her old bedroom. She must have fallen asleep immediately because she remembered nothing after settling into the bed.

"Christine? Are you awake?"

Sliding her feet into the slippers Melinda had left, Christine grabbed the matching robe off the bed and scuffed her way across the room. She stretched and yawned as she opened the door.

"What plans? I have to get into the office. What time is Henry leaving?"

Melinda slipped past her, walked to the window and pushed the drapes aside. "It's a beautiful day. I've set the table on the patio. You still have clothes in the closet. Pick something light because it's already warm."

She was gone in a flash, leaving Christine with a bad feeling. She dressed quickly and hurried down the stairs and out to the patio. With a sinking heart she noted the two place settings. "Where is Henry?"

Melinda's eyes filled with understanding and concern. "Oh, honey. I'm sorry. Henry left an hour ago. But don't you worry. We're going to have a fabulous day."

Christine sagged into a chair as Melinda's words sank in. Henry was serious. He was not letting her work.

Melinda chattered on, something about a spa day, but Christine tuned out. She had more serious concerns. If Henry was not going to let her return to work, what was she going to do?

Work wasn't just a job. It was her life. So much of what she had planned depended on being employed in the US Attorney's Office. Her goal for as long as she could remember had been to become a lawyer and uphold her mother's legacy. To fulfill that dream, she had to be able to work. Her fingers clenched the handle of the mug Melinda had set before her. She couldn't give in to this. She had to fight back.

"Christine?"

"Yes?"

"Good. I'll go reserve places for us. You're going to love the hot-stone massage. Finish your coffee. I'll be back."

What? Christine watched Melinda walk toward the

house and wondered what she'd agreed to. Whatever it was, she'd find a way out. There was only one thing she was going to focus on today—getting to the bottom of what she had witnessed yesterday.

A breeze blew her napkin off the table, and Christine bent to pick it up. Her head was still below the table when a shot rang out, and a bullet shattered the glass back of her chair.

For a moment, shock paralyzed Christine. Was someone actually shooting at her? Again?

The sound of another shot taking out the umbrella jolted her to action. She slid the rest of the way out of the chair and flattened herself on the patio stones. *Breathe. Calm down. Think.*

This had to be related to the murder she had witnessed yesterday. Why else would someone be shooting at her in a private backyard? What could she do?

She had no weapon to defend herself, so she had to stay focused and use her brain. Lifting her head a fraction, she studied her surroundings, particularly the elaborate grill pit Henry had installed. For once she was happy with how seriously the man took his barbeque. He had essentially built an outdoor kitchen complete with fireplace, smoker and a bricked-in island for eating.

The island was closest, and hiding behind it seemed like the best way to get out of the direct line of fire. She slithered her way over the flagstones until she reached the relative safety of the solid structure.

Resting her back against the brick, she sucked in a breath and took stock. The island provided good cover and temporary safety, but it allowed no view of what was happening. She had no idea where the shooter was and no way to call for help. Essentially, she was a sitting duck unless she could get Melinda's attention.

Pressing herself to the ground, she peered around the edge of the island. The house provided the only real safety, but between her and the sliding glass doors stretched the pool and a lot of empty space. If she could only reach her phone, but it lay glistening in the sun on the table where moments earlier she'd been sitting.

Her gaze moved from the table to the shattered chair back, and terror rose in her throat. If not for the breeze blowing her napkin…

Her pulse pounded in her neck, and her body started to shake uncontrollably, but she forced herself to think. God came to Elijah in a whisper on the wind. Had He come to her on a breeze, reassuring her He was here for her? Assuring her she was not alone?

Huddled behind the island, she uttered a prayer of thanksgiving and focused on what to do next. It wasn't like she had many alternatives, and the longer she held off the shooter, the greater the chance Melinda would come back. Why hadn't she returned yet? It was taking her an awfully long time to make an appointment. Maybe the air-conditioning and sealed-up house had prevented her from hearing, or maybe she'd heard the gunfire and was calling for help.

Christine knew she needed to buy time. Remembering the threat from yesterday, she called out in desperation. "You're wasting your time, risking your life for nothing. I didn't see anything. I don't know who you are."

Another blast took out a jar of flowers sitting on the island. Shards of glass showered around her, forcing her to acknowledge that giving away her position may not have been the smartest move.

Should she make a run for it?

Another round of shots decided her. This situation called for action.

She thought back to the moment she'd stepped out onto the patio. She'd noticed there were glass jars of flowers on either end of the island. The one above her was shattered, but if she could grab the other one, she could throw it as a distraction.

Sidling along the wall, she waited until she was fairly sure she was equidistant from where the first jar had been. Melinda tended to be precise in her decorations.

Keeping her body below the island top, Christine reached up and slid her hand along the counter. She rose on her knees until she could grab it, but just as she started to slide the jar toward her, it shattered in her hand.

She dropped quickly to the patio and breathed in to slow her racing heart. That shot had come from a different direction. Did that mean he'd changed position or that there was more than one of them? Either way, she was truly trapped now.

No! She could not let them defeat her. She would not be a helpless victim. She had to take control. Which was laughable given that they had guns.

But she knew the house and patio layout. She couldn't let panic steal that advantage. There was a woodpile next to the fireplace. If she could distract them and get behind it, she'd have an easy dash to the pool house and shelter.

Think, Christine. There had to be something to use. Henry kept his cooking tools in a drawer in the is-

land. She almost laughed, remembering that and thinking how upset he'd be at her using them. He'd just have
to deal.

She grabbed the spatula and flung it across the patio.
A split second later, she sent the tongs flying in the opposite direction while she rolled the third way behind
the tower of wood. Panting, she stayed flat while they
belatedly shot at the woodpile, sending chips scattering around her.

There was no way she was going to be able to get to
the house, but at least now she was closer to the pool
house. There was a phone in there, and Henry had installed bullet-resistant windows after a hunter had accidentally shot onto the property a few years ago. But
would they fall for a distraction a second time?

Before she could finish formulating the plan, the
back door opened, and Melinda started out. "Christine?"

"Get back. There's someone shooting out here."

Melinda froze in the doorway, so Christine screamed
again. "Go inside. Call 911."

A round blasted off the shutters beside the door. Melinda ducked inside, and Christine could only pray she'd
get help quickly. The danger had just become more immediate. The shooters knew police were on the way, but
it would take time for them to arrive. If they intended to
take her out, they'd have to make a move soon.

Almost as confirmation, a barrage of shots hit the
woodpile from both directions, scattering logs and de-
stroying her protection.

Divine inspiration calmed her. She took the biggest
piece of wood she could reach and hurled it toward the
pool house. The second it left her hands, she dashed in

the same direction and dove behind the lounge chair, then rolled into the overflow moat around the back side of the pool.

Peace flooded her as shots were fired in the opposite direction. She'd been right. They didn't fall for the same trick twice, so she'd outplayed them. The moat wouldn't provide cover for long, but she could crouch and run for the building. Every minute she bought hopefully brought the police closer.

Bullets kicked up waves in the pool, and Christine felt the water splash as she launched herself out of the moat and behind the building.

Return shots drew her attention. What was happening?

She dared a glance around the corner only to see Melinda shooting from behind the shattered door with Henry's hunting rifle.

Apparently, the first round of shots cued the men into Melinda's excellent marksmanship. Coupled with the scream of approaching sirens, it sent them running for the back fence.

Christine's legs gave way and she sagged against the wall. It was over. She was safe. For now.

Christine's message had been garbled and semi-hysterical, so Blake wasn't clear exactly what had happened. As he raced to the house, he clung to the one word he'd clearly made out. Safe. She was safe.

Squad cars filled the driveway and blocked the front of the house, but the door stood wide-open. Blake flashed ID at the officer standing guard and entered the living room.

The scene that met his eyes stopped him in his

tracks. The US Attorney stood with his arm around a woman on one side of the room, but Christine sat huddled in the corner of a sofa, swaddled in an afghan, as a detective interviewed her.

The gaze she lifted to meet his revealed shell-shocked green eyes. Her face was pale, and she looked like she was withdrawing into herself.

By contrast, the woman was smiling at the man and one of the police officers. Blake could make out the man teasing something about her ranch girl upbringing and how she was a handy person to have around in a pinch. She gave a nervous laugh that set his nerves on edge. What had happened here?

Blake glanced back at Christine. He wanted to rush to her side and offer comfort, but professional courtesy held him back. The detective must have noticed her reaction to him though, because he turned to look at Blake. He was visibly irritated at the interruption, but rose anyway.

Blake stepped forward and extended his hand. "Ranger Blake Larsen. I didn't mean to disrupt your interview, Detective. I just stopped by to check on Ms. Davis."

The detective eyed him warily. "You know Ms. Davis?"

Blake turned a wide smile on Christine. "We're acquainted." He turned back to the detective. "If I might have just a moment?"

At the detective's nod, he stepped in front of the man and knelt in front of Christine, taking her hands into his. They were blocks of ice.

He moved quickly onto the sofa and wrapped his arm around her shoulder. Immediately, he felt the damp from her clothes seeping through the afghan and into his own. Had no one had the presence of mind to get her dry clothes?

"What happened here?" His voice sounded harsh, but too bad if anyone was offended.

The detective seemed to weigh his options, and finally responded with the respect due a colleague. "Ms. Davis was shot at in the backyard. I was in the process of getting the details when you arrived."

"Can it wait until someone gets her some dry clothes?"

Christine, seemingly bolstered by his appearance, rested a hand on his arm. "It's okay. I did change. It's my hair dripping. If someone could just get me a towel, I'll be fine."

Fine seemed a stretch to Blake, but he rose to get a towel. By the time he returned, the detective had resumed questioning her. Blake handed her the towel and took a seat on a chair that was out of the detective's line of vision but within hearing range. From this vantage point he could still observe Christine, and more importantly, she could feel his support—something she obviously needed.

Despite appearing physically unharmed, she looked… Well, *shattered* was the only word that came to mind. And how would she not be? She'd been the target of gunmen twice in two days.

As he observed the interview, unease settled in Blake's gut. The detective was thorough in his questioning, but it was the angle of the questions that troubled him. If he was reading her correctly, Christine was bothered, too. The detective had moved on from facts about the attack, to seeking possible motivation for it, with no mention of the incident she had witnessed yesterday. All his attention seemed focused on her caseload in the US Attorney's Office. Was there anyone who had threatened her? Anyone who seemed particularly resentful?

"Detective, every criminal I put behind bars is resentful."

"Any family members that seemed inclined towards revenge?" he persisted.

"No. As far as I know, the only people who want me dead are the ones who murdered a man in front of me yesterday."

"Duly noted." He cleared his throat and continued. "Have there been any victims or family members who considered that you let them down by not getting a conviction?"

Christine abruptly stood up and stared down at him. "That would also be no. If you have no further questions…"

The detective also stood, but his gaze did not meet Christine's. He looked down at his notepad, and Blake could feel his unease. Something was not right. Why was he not pursuing the point Christine had made about yesterday's murder?

"I have nothing else at the moment. I'll get back to you if I do."

He walked over to join the other group. Although Blake couldn't hear much of the conversation, he could make out enough to realize the detective was going to take the woman's statement.

"That's my boss, Henry, and his wife, Melinda. I wonder if he'll ask her about unsatisfied customers."

Blake looked back at Christine, who had pulled the

afghan tightly around her shoulders, resentment clear on her face.

"What's going on here, Ranger Larsen? Why are they pretending yesterday didn't happen?"

Blake wished he had a response to satisfy her. "I was hoping you knew that answer."

She studied him for a moment. "And what about you? Are you also going to deny I witnessed a murder yesterday?"

Blake sensed a lot was hanging on his answer, so he thought carefully about what to say.

Before he could formulate his reply, she shrugged. "I see," she murmured, and started to walk away.

"Wait."

She turned back, and the expectant look on her face touched something deep within him. "I believe you."

There. Saying the words to her sent a rush of relief cascading through him, washing away the tension that nagged at him. "I believe you." He glanced around the room. "But I don't think this is the place to talk about it."

She faced him, head held high, as if his words had infused her with a renewed confidence. "Then please get me out of here and take me somewhere we can talk."

FOUR

Getting Christine out of the house was easier said than done. Blake's attempts at reason with Henry failed, so he turned his argument to Melinda. "She needs to get away from the house. Away from all this." He gestured to the crime scene techs set up on the patio.

"Where do you plan to take her?" Henry demanded.

Blake bristled but reminded himself that if their roles were reversed, he'd react the same. "My brother, also a Texas Ranger, owns a ranch near Cedar Creek. She can get some air and relax a bit. He has state-of-the-art security. She'll be safe there."

Melinda laid a hand on Henry's arm. "Let her go. He's a Texas Ranger. She'll be fine."

Blake turned back to look at Christine, wondering how she was reacting to these people making decisions for her. Her demeanor scared him. She was retreating into herself again. He could almost see her shutting down before his eyes. He guessed Melinda saw it, too, because she walked over to Christine and gently urged her to go with her and change into drier clothing.

While she was gone Blake seized the opportunity to confront Henry and the detective. "Why aren't you considering the shooting yesterday as possible motive for this morning's attack?"

Henry glared at him. "If you're supporting her in that ridiculous claim, then I'm rethinking whether she should go with you."

Blake heaved a mental sigh and reminded himself of his promise to his boss. Rather than give in to his anger at Henry, he needed to get to the root of his response. "Has Ms. Davis recanted her claim?"

"No." Henry bit the word out.

"Then why don't you believe her?"

"Did you miss the news bulletin that no body was found?"

Blake stuffed his hands in his pockets, trying to look casual while he made sure he could see both men's faces as he responded. "I did read that report. I also know how much time elapsed between the shooting and my call to the police after Ms. Davis told me about it. There was more than enough time for a body to be removed."

Henry remained stoic, but Blake detected a glimmer of something in his eyes. The detective merely shrugged. "I saw nothing at the warehouse to indicate anything amiss. If you know something different, Ranger, feel free to file a report."

"Be careful they don't take away your job for imagining it."

A revitalized Christine stood in the doorway, fists clenched, her face a mask of defiant anger. Whatever had happened upstairs, he was grateful to Melinda for helping.

"Christine, please." Henry walked toward her.

She stood her ground, and Blake felt a flash of admiration. This was the woman whose reputation he knew.

"Please what, Henry? You've known me all my life. You know I'm not given to flights of fancy. I'm telling you that I witnessed a murder yesterday, and you are dismissing me simply because there was no body found an hour later? I don't even know how to process that."

She walked past him and approached Blake. "I'd like to leave now."

Blake had nothing more to say to Henry, either, but he did have a lot of investigating to do. Getting Christine safely to his brother's ranch was the first step. As he took her arm and escorted her to the door, he could feel her body trembling, and he realized what the show of strength had cost her.

He had her wait in the shelter of the house while he pulled his truck up the drive. When he got out and opened her door, he kept careful watch in all directions. Once she was inside and the door was closed, he walked back around, scouting the street to make sure there was no danger. By the time he climbed in, she had shrunk into the corner. Blake's heart hurt.

"If you don't feel safe, we can go back inside."

She shook her head. "I don't feel safe in a place where no one believes me."

Blake ached to press for answers about Henry's reaction, but this was not the time. He wanted to be able to give her his full attention for that discussion, so he forced himself to wait and asked a different question.

"What *do* you want?"

She looked up, and the pain and despair in her eyes ripped through him. "I want someone to believe me. I want to be able to prove I didn't imagine the murder." She sank her head onto her chest. "I want my life back."

"Hey…" He waited until she looked at him again. "I

believe you, my boss believes you and the Texas Rangers are going to give you your life back."

She shrugged. "You can't promise that."

He couldn't. He shouldn't. He did, anyway. "That's why I'm taking you to Dylan's ranch. We're going to do our own investigation."

His promise probably didn't quite justify the spark he'd put back in her eyes, but he vowed to do whatever it took to keep it there.

"Your brother is also a Ranger?"

Blake nodded. "Dylan's a Ranger now. Our dad was a Ranger." He turned and smiled at her. "I guess you could say it's our family business."

She smiled back, but there was a sad tinge to hers. "My mother was an assistant US attorney, also. I guess the law is our family business."

He picked up on the past tense. "Is she retired?"

"She was murdered when I was a child. Henry and Melinda took me in and raised me. Maybe that's why he is focusing on my cases. Mom was working on a case with him when she was killed. They were trying to bring down a cartel."

"He survived?" That was one more fact to tally in the suspicious column.

"He wasn't with her that night. I think he was out of town. She was working late and was ambushed on her way home."

"I'm sorry." Blake knew what it was like to grow up without a mother. The difference was his had left willingly. He cleared his throat. Now was not the time to think about his mother, either. His focus had to stay on keeping Christine safe from the men who were obviously not giving up.

* * *

Blake put on music that helped soothe her, and Christine found herself drifting in and out of sleep as they drove. It amazed her that she'd known him for less than twenty-four hours. In that short time, he'd shown her more respect and care than people she'd known her entire life.

While she'd been changing clothes, Melinda had teased about going off with her handsome Ranger. Christine couldn't deny the handsome part, but his faith in her appealed to her far more than his good looks. A man who stood by a person was invaluable. That was the lesson she'd learned from her mother and grandmother, both of whom had been failed by the men they'd loved.

Christine stared out the truck window as the suburbs gave way to ranch land. Spring was on the verge of bursting out. Soon these fields would be bursting with bluebonnets and Indian paintbrush.

Would she be alive to enjoy them?

The insidious question sent a shudder through her.

Blake reached over and caught her hand, giving it a squeeze. "We're almost there."

A short time later they drove through the gates of his brother's ranch.

"Don't let the rustic look deceive you," Blake commented. "Dylan's work has made him a bit paranoid about security. His system is top-notch."

Christine smiled. "After my morning, I'm grateful for his paranoia."

A slightly taller, slightly older version of Blake was waiting on the front porch when they drove up to the sprawling house. He ambled down the steps and came over to open her door.

"Ms. Davis, I presume." He doffed his cowboy hat. "Welcome to my home."

Christine took his proffered hand, and he helped her down from the truck. "Thank you, Ranger Larsen."

He smiled at her. "Just call me Dylan. Too many Ranger Larsens in this family to stick on formality."

"Thank you, Dylan." She stood tall and breathed in deeply. The fresh spring air filled her lungs and lifted her spirits. "I don't know if Blake had a chance to explain why we're here, but I'm grateful to you for having me."

Blake came up beside them. "I gave him a quick version. I wanted him to hear the details straight from your mouth."

Dylan ushered them into the house, heading straight back to a large kitchen that looked out on vast grazing land. "When Blake said he was bringing you, I rustled up some lunch. Why don't we talk while we eat?"

Christine eyed the platter of enchiladas. "You just *rustled* this up?"

Dylan shrugged modestly. "A man learns to cook if he wants to eat."

Christine smiled again, more warmly this time. She was growing to like these brothers more with every passing moment, which brought to mind the question that had nagged at her. She waited until they were seated and Dylan had said a blessing over the food.

She took a few bites, and even complimented Dylan on his cooking, but then she couldn't restrain herself. "I have a question."

Blake eyed her steadily. "I think we all have questions."

"That's partly what mine is about."

He waited attentively, so she continued. "Honestly, I'm puzzled. I'm not even sure how to ask this, so I'm just going to come out and say it. Why are you helping me?"

Blake shrugged. "You needed help."

She glanced from him to Dylan, who also shrugged and nodded before digging back into his food. Was it that simple? They saw someone in need and rushed to help? They were Texas Rangers, after all.

She rested her hands on the table and met his gaze. "You just help anyone who needs it?"

"You're not just anyone."

Christine smiled self-consciously. "I get that I probably sounded pretty frantic when I called you."

Dylan snickered.

When Blake threw him a warning look, Christine laughed. "I might have overreacted, but—"

Blake interrupted her. "You had two attempts on your life in as many days. I think you're entitled." He held her gaze. "But I also think you're asking something more than why I came to the house when you called."

"I am." She fiddled with her bracelet, rolling it around her wrist. "Nearly running someone down, through no fault of your own, is no one's idea of fun. I get that. And I understand you wanting to make sure I'm okay. But helping me now is not requisite payment. I probably shouldn't have called you. You already saved my life." She shrugged her confusion. "So, yes. I have to wonder why you came when I called, why you're willing to involve yourself and your brother when no one in law enforcement believes me."

Blake rested his hands on the wood-plank table, and she noted the stark contrast between his skin and the crisp white cotton where his sleeves were rolled back. They were strong hands, capable looking, deeply tanned, as were his arms and face. Features of a man who spent his days outdoors as much as in.

Blake cleared his throat, and her attention jolted back.

"Fair question." He closed his eyes a moment and leaned his head back against his chair. When he opened his eyes, he met her questioning gaze head-on. "It comes down to this. I don't understand why a prosecutor with your sterling reputation is being dismissed so easily." His fingers pressed down into the wood of the table, and she felt the tension, the truth of his statement.

Christine studied his face, trying to gauge his expression. What she saw inspired confidence, but was it justified? What did she know of this man other than the fact that he had saved her life by not hitting her with his car? That he said he wanted to help? In her desperation, what was she risking by placing her trust in him?

"You don't know me, Christine. But it's okay to trust that I want to help you." He grinned. "I'm not reading your thoughts. It's a normal question.

"I'm a Texas Ranger. We're taught to investigate anything unusual, anything suspicious." He took a deep breath and exhaled harshly before continuing. "Everything about this case bothers me. It's all suspicious. Look, I could understand if some vagrant had reported the body or even if you were a questionable witness. But you're a colleague, a trusted member of the law enforcement community. The fact that they are not taking your claim seriously sets off my radar."

Unexpected warmth washed over Christine. A sense of validation, affirmation that maybe she wasn't losing it. With his words, he'd given her back yet another part of herself. Strengthened her.

"Thank you."

He humbled her with his praise, but his point was exactly what unnerved her. More specifically, she feared to contemplate why Henry, who should have known and trusted her more than anyone, chose to ignore the truth.

Another truth slithered through her mind. With the killers still after her, *she* couldn't ignore it. Her life was at stake. If law enforcement wouldn't properly investigate, she would have to do it herself—hopefully, with Blake's help.

"It makes no sense to me. But I need to figure it out if I want to be safe."

"I understand. That's why Dylan and I are here to help you. We have the full backing of the Rangers."

Relief coursed through Christine, draining some of the tension that bound her. She closed her eyes and tried to clear her brain. She needed focus. When she opened them, she found Dylan and Blake patiently waiting. She turned to Blake. "I don't know if you've already told Dylan, but will you tell me what happened when you called the police?"

Blake nodded, and she watched him sift through his memories. Listening to him and observing him reinforced her sense that he was an excellent Ranger, as well as a kind man.

"After I left you, I called in the shooting. I told them what occurred when you ran in front of my car, and I explained what you told me about there being a deceased person in the building."

Christine shuddered at his words.

He gave her a moment to compose herself before continuing. "Dispatch said they would send a unit to investigate."

"Do you have any idea how long it took for someone to get there?"

"I know exactly how long. I was waiting when they arrived."

Christine's eyes widened. "You went back?"

"For all the good it did me." He took a sip of his water and toyed with the food on his plate. "They took their sweet time getting there. I was really tempted to go in myself."

Christine didn't have to ask why he didn't. It was all about jurisdiction. "Would you have any reason to think they were waiting for specific officers or were intentionally delaying?"

Blake racked up points for seeing immediately where she was going with that. His eyes narrowed, and he studied her a moment before responding. "Do you have any reason to suspect corruption?"

Christine sat back in her chair and raised her eyes to the ceiling, carefully considering her words before speaking. She sighed. "I have no specific reason." She rubbed her finger along the edge of her bracelet. "But I've been around law enforcement my entire life. I know there are pressures. I know things happen."

Blake exchanged looks with his brother before responding. "I can't argue that. I've seen good men brought low by family problems and financial pressures." He shook his head sadly. "I've also known the cartels to turn men I never would have believed possible."

He drummed his fingers lightly on the tablecloth. "But, to answer your question, was there a delay? Did the responding officer contact a specific colleague? Honestly, I can't say for sure. It did feel like it took too long for backup to arrive, but they mentioned something about there being a lot of traffic accidents due to the storm. I knew how bad driving conditions had been, so it didn't strike me as suspicious…until there was no body."

No body. Those two words haunted her. She knew she'd seen a man die. What could possibly have happened afterward? She clung to the only possibility— that someone had removed the body during the delay. It was the only explanation that made sense—if any of this made sense—but it didn't solve her immediate problem. Someone wanted her dead.

She bit down on her lip, forced herself to relax. When she spoke, her words were calm but resolute. "You're not going to like this, but I want to go back there."

"There being…?"

"The building where I witnessed the murder."

"I really don't think it's a good idea, Christine."

She laughed though the laughter was tinged with frustration. "I know it's not. But I need to do it."

"Why?"

She pushed her chair back and rose to pace the kitchen. "For some reason I don't understand, the police and Henry are convinced nothing happened yesterday and that today's shooting was job related."

She walked to the window and stood looking out at

the cattle grazing peacefully in the sun. If only her life could be that serene again.

She turned back, and resignation etched her face. "I don't know if corruption is involved or if they really believe I imagined this. It almost doesn't matter. If they insist on focusing on my past cases, they stand no chance of apprehending the men who shot at me."

She shivered. "I can still hear the man's voice in my head. 'We can't take a chance. Find her.' Obviously they're still after me, and it seems apparent they're not going to stop until I'm dead."

She drew herself up straight. "That leaves me no choice. I need to find them first. It's the only chance I have to stay alive. And I need your help."

FIVE

Another woman was relying on him to keep her alive.

Momentary panic rippled through Blake. He wanted to warn Christine that he wasn't worthy of her confidence.

Except he had been promising her that he would do exactly what she was asking.

Dylan caught his eye, and Blake could see his brother reading his reaction. A subtle shake of his head was his brother's only sign that he understood, but it settled Blake. He took a breath and exhaled slowly. Christine was not like Sofia, the woman in his last case. She was not an abused spouse with conflicted loyalties.

And he was a Texas Ranger, trained and prepared for exactly these kinds of circumstances. Sofia's case would haunt him for the rest of his life. He would carry her death in his heart, but in his mind he knew it did not reflect on his ability as a Ranger. Christine Davis was a professional, a dedicated law enforcement official who was not afraid to stand up for what was right. She deserved someone equally strong and committed to stand beside her. She deserved support from people who believed in her. He and Dylan could provide that.

That did not mean he had to agree to her plan to be involved in the investigation; however, looking at the defiant expression on her face, he decided this was not the time for that argument.

"I don't like the idea of going back there, but I understand why it feels necessary." Blake turned to his brother. "What do you think?"

Dylan looked at Christine. "I'd prefer you let us do this without you."

When Christine started to protest, Dylan interrupted her. "But I think it would be beneficial to visit the scene with you and let you walk us through it. I think we can do that safely if you promise to follow our rules."

At Christine's nod, Blake spoke again. "We can drive in separate cars and head down to the crime scene together. When we're finished there, I'll drive you back to Henry and Melinda's house for the night."

Christine let out a sigh of relief. "Thank you."

Blake scrubbed his hands over his face. He could only hope she'd still be thanking him later.

Dylan led the way in his car with Blake and Christine following behind in the truck. There was no sign of anything suspicious as Dylan turned onto the block where Blake had narrowly avoided hitting Christine, but just seeing the road gave Blake flashbacks. He could only imagine how Christine felt. He fought an urge to put an arm around her shoulder and checked in verbally, instead. "Are you okay?"

The wide eyes she turned on him proved he'd been correct. She was struggling with revisiting the scene. "We can leave," he offered gently.

She stiffened her shoulders and held her head high. "No, I've got this."

They got out of the car, and Blake walked with Christine while Dylan followed behind, keeping watch. Christine began to narrate as she walked. "I was coming along in this direction when the wind first began to whip up. My phone blared an alarm. Thunder and lightning were really close." She shuddered. "I was too far from my car, so I was looking for someplace to take shelter. As you can see, there's no other real choice, so I ducked under the scaffolding here..." Her voice trailed off.

"What's wrong?"

"This." Christine pointed at the shiny new padlock. "That was definitely not there yesterday. The door was ajar. I waited under the scaffolding at first, but when the storm grew worse, I ducked inside. That's when I heard the voices and witnessed the murder." She looked from Blake to Dylan. "Who would have put the padlock on?"

"Someone who doesn't want the building disturbed."

"Interesting there's a new lock, but no crime scene tape," Dylan added as Blake crouched to study the padlock.

"Because no one believes I witnessed a crime."

Blake heard the discouragement in her voice, and he couldn't bear the broken look on her face. "Hey. We believe you, and we're not giving up this easily."

Christine shook her head. "The padlock changes things. I can't very well ask Texas Rangers to break into a building and trespass. We need a warrant." She gave a harsh laugh. "And who is going to issue a warrant if no one believes a crime was committed?"

Much as he hated to admit it, Blake knew she was right. This was a dead end. The lack of crime scene tape coupled with a shiny padlock was the most telling evidence they'd get today. They needed a different plan—one that got them away from here.

Dylan echoed his thoughts. "Let's go. You take Christine home, and I'll call some friends, see what I can find out."

They strode quickly back to the parked cars, tension building with every step. Agreeing to bring Christine here had been a mistake. He knew it in his gut.

Blake was still second-guessing himself ten minutes later as he drove along the highway. A flash of light off a mirror caught his attention.

"When you took shelter in the warehouse yesterday, did you notice any trucks parked outside?"

"I can't say I really noticed. I was too preoccupied with getting out of the storm." She studied him. "Why?"

"We might have picked up a tail. Don't look," he warned as she swiveled. "Check in the side-view mirror. See if you recognize it."

Christine glanced in the mirror at the truck several car lengths back. It matched about a dozen other trucks on the road. Dusty, hard-driven. "Can't say I know it."

"Okay, just stay down. I'm going to act like we suspect nothing, and see what they do." Tension hummed in the air, but he maintained speed as the car continued down the highway. Either the tail would prove real and he'd have to take evasive action, or it was just a truck heading in the same direction. He hoped for the latter, but his instincts were screaming tail.

When the other driver veered off down a side street, the release of tension was palpable. "Looks like we're okay."

In a slightly lighter mood, he followed Christine's directions to Henry's house. "How much longer are you planning on staying here?" he asked as he pulled up the drive.

"I don't know. I'd prefer to return to my own place." She fidgeted a moment before adding, "Like I said before, it's hard staying where no one believes you. But I'm not stupid. Going home to my apartment with inadequate security is too risky."

"Agreed. You're safer here."

Christine gave a short laugh. "Ironic, isn't it?"

She rested her hand on the door latch, then suddenly turned and faced him. "May I ask you something else?"

He nodded, matching her solemn expression with his own.

"We've danced around this a bit, but I need to come right out and ask. Does it bother you that Henry denies I saw someone get murdered? That he would believe that rather than me?"

Blake swallowed hard. "That's a loaded question."

She acknowledged it with a nod as she visibly struggled to keep the pain from showing. "Henry refuses to hear anything I have to say about it. He seems absolutely certain I'm wrong."

She paused there, but Blake didn't really have an answer. "What are you thinking?"

"I don't know. I've been mulling it over all day. I came up with two possibilities. The first is he's trying to protect me."

"From what?"

"It goes back a ways. My mother and Henry were good friends all their lives. They went through law school together, joined the US Attorney's Office together, made their careers together." She fidgeted with her bracelet, struggling to say the next words.

"As I said earlier, my mother was killed because of a case they were working on. Henry and Melinda took me into their family, raised me alongside their children." She let out a sigh. "He's always been protective."

She looked away and cleared her throat. "Henry was not happy about my choice to follow in my mother's footsteps. He tried to talk me out of it, but when I stood firm, he came around. He's been my rock ever since, supporting my career every step of the way." She shook her head and shrugged. "I can only hope he's acting this way now because he's worried about me."

"What is the other possibility you came up with?"

"That he is somehow involved."

Christine wished she could bite back the words the minute they escaped her lips. She absolutely hated that they'd even crossed her mind. Uttering them aloud was wrong. Accusing Henry of corruption was unthinkable.

"I'm sorry. Forget I said that. I'm sure it's his misguided attempt to protect me from myself."

Blake looked like he wanted to pursue it, then he shrugged. "Why would he need to protect you from yourself?"

Christine sighed. There was no good way to answer that. Doubt nagged at her. If she admitted the validity of Henry's concerns, what would Blake think? Would he agree with Henry that she was having an emotional breakdown? Would admitting her failings make him less likely to believe in her?

Christine rested her hands in her lap so he couldn't see how tensely they were clasped. She closed her eyes, reminded herself to breathe, and then she opened her eyes and angled her head to look directly at him. She couldn't be anything less than truthful.

"I wasn't trying to hide anything from you and Dylan. I just don't really know how to talk about it. I've had… some problems recently…with anxiety… It started with a kidnapping attempt involving a case. It was mistaken identity." She shrugged. "They were trying to grab my witness but snatched me instead. I got away. We caught them, prosecuted the case. They're all behind bars." She drew in another breath and, feeling stronger, continued. "That had nothing to do with my current caseload. Yes, I've been fighting anxiety, but there's been absolutely nothing to indicate I would imagine nonexistent murders. I was fine until the rain started. I was coming from one meeting and heading to another. I was in a hurry, I had a million things on my mind."

As she spoke, her confidence resurged. "I absolutely did not imagine any of this."

She bit down on her lip, forced herself to relax. When she spoke, her words were calm but resolute. "There *was* a body. I'd stake my life on it."

Blake didn't say anything, so she continued on. "I hate this, you know. Hate having to prove I'm okay. Hate that people who should believe me don't. I may suffer from anxiety attacks, but I'm not a quitter. And if they think they can scare me off, they're dead wrong."

Blake studied her for a long moment. "Okay."

Christine waited as the silence stretched out. "That's it?"

He shrugged. "I can grill you if you want, but I'm a pretty good judge of character, and I have no reason to doubt you."

She scrunched up her face. "There is that little matter of the missing body."

"Oh, that."

She laughed, and it sounded as freeing as it felt. She hadn't realized until that moment how much she was relying on his offer of help or how much she feared he would withdraw it. "Please don't tell me this happens all the time."

Blake raised an eyebrow. "Probably more than you think. Historically, there are hundreds of convictions for murder with no body being found."

Christine sagged back against the seat. "Those numbers should be reassuring, but they terrify me."

"Why?"

"No one in law enforcement other than you and Dylan believes I witnessed a murder. That means no one but us is looking for a murderer."

Blake looked troubled. "That's true."

"But the murderers are still looking for me."

Awkward silence hung between them. Blake wanted to reassure her, but she was too smart to be pacified by empty promises. He cleared his throat. "I know I haven't really been much help so far, but let me look into things tonight. I'll have a better plan in the morning. I'll call you."

"I'd like that."

Her response was so awkward that they both burst out laughing. "Sorry, that made it sound like I was accepting a date."

Tension thrummed again.

"It would be the most unusual date I'd ever had." He let the words tail off and just smiled at her.

She smiled back. "I really do appreciate all that you're doing to help me. I know you must have more important things to focus on than the foolish woman who ran in front of your car."

Blake shook his head. "Let's get this out of the way, Christine. I'm not doing this because you ran in front of my car. You witnessed a crime. I believe that. I believe you. And my job is investigating crimes. So, if it makes you feel better, think of it as helping me do my job."

"But—"

"No buts. Think about it tonight if you can. Maybe you'll come up with some detail you forgot."

Think about it if she could. As if she could think about anything else. Christine waited as he came around to open her door. His gentlemanly care was unnerving her because, if she was honest, she was enjoying his company far more than just doing a job.

When they reached the front door, she turned to face him. "I'm good from here."

"Trying to keep me from picking a fight with Henry?" he teased.

"More like trying to protect you from Melinda's matchmaking schemes."

He chuckled. "Go on in alone. I'll watch from here."

She put her hand on the door and paused. "Thank you. Your support means the world to me."

He doffed his hat. "My pleasure, ma'am." He winked.

Once she was inside, Blake walked slowly back to his truck, his gaze sweeping the lawn and street. Twilight was settling gently over the peaceful neighborhood, but there was nothing peaceful or gentle about the anxiety churning in his gut. He was aware of the background noise—dogs barking, children's voices calling to each other—but the normal sounds were subdued by the worries echoing through his brain.

He could put it down to roused nerves from the truck he'd thought was tailing them earlier, but it was more than that. Something was seriously off about this whole situation, and he didn't like the idea of leaving Christine here.

According to the message he'd received earlier, Henry had had his security system upgraded this afternoon, and police were stepping up patrols in the neighborhood.

That should have reassured him, but it didn't. Probably because it was clear they were still focused on investigating cases in the US Attorney's Office as the source of the attacks. Under normal circumstances, that was the obvious choice, but when you had one of your star prosecutors claiming she witnessed what sounded like an execution, normal protocol should have dictated widening the investigation. That no one seemed inclined to do so just heightened his sense of unease. He put the truck in gear and backed down the drive.

What had Christine walked into yesterday? Why was it being deliberately ignored or, worse, covered up? How could he keep her alive?

The obvious answer was she should be in a safe house somewhere until this was resolved. In fact, he would put in a call to his boss about that right now. It was time for an update, and that would also give him an excuse to pull over and watch the house from a distance.

He'd barely cut the ignition when his phone rang.

"You're not very good at undercover work, are you?"

Blake pictured her at a window watching him and laughed. "Made me, did you?"

Her return laughter sent a cascade of joy through his body. He liked her.

"I told you I'd be fine. I'm an assistant United States attorney. I'm used to dealing with some pretty tough guys, Blake."

Blake stifled a groan. "So, are you going to make me sit here in the car, or—"

His voice broke as he saw a dusty truck make a turn on to the block.

"Christine." He tried to keep his voice steady to avoid panicking her. "Where are you?"

"In the living room with Henry and Melinda."

The truck headed slowly up the street. Blake's nerves tingled. "Is there something you can hide behind?"

"Why?" Her laughing question cut off as she registered the tone of his voice. "What is it, Blake? You're scaring me. What's wrong?"

The change in her voice was instant. The quaver that belied all her brave front broke his heart. "The truck that followed us is driving down the street. It's moving slowly, but it's almost there."

The barrel of a gun emerged from the car window.

"Christine. Get down now. Get everyone down now. Someone is about to open fire on the house."

He could hear her repeating his warning, hear the arguments.

"Get down! Get flat now!"

As he was talking, Blake started the car and headed toward the truck, but there was less distance between her and the truck than between his car and her. "I'm coming, but you need to get down now."

He gunned the car, but even as he picked up speed, he knew there was no way he could reach her in time. He was still a hundred yards away when a hail of bullets poured out the truck window with the awful sound playing in stereo through her phone and live before his eyes.

SIX

Fear and rage coursed through Blake. "Christine? Can you hear me?"

Silence.

"Chris, answer me."

The truck roared past him, and his own back window shattered as the shooter turned the gun on him. He slid down the seat and slammed on the brakes.

For half a second he considered pursuing the attackers, but the silence from Christine's phone changed his mind. He skidded to a stop in front of the house, threw the car into Park and jumped out. He snapped a quick photo of the receding truck with his phone, hoping to catch a license plate, but it was probably too far away now.

He turned toward the house and his heart sank. The huge picture window in Henry's living room was shattered. The shrill sound of the house alarm underscored the terror in Blake's heart. A lot of good it had done.

For the second time in as many days, he ran toward Christine. Again his heart was in his throat, but this time his reaction was personal.

"Christine!" He shouted her name as he raced across

the manicured lawn. "Christine!" He pounded on the front door. "It's Blake. Can you hear me? They're gone. Let me in."

Henry opened the door a crack. "They can hear you two counties over," he grumbled.

One look at his shell-shocked face, and Blake easily forgave the gruff response. He pushed past the man. "Christine. Is she okay?"

Henry pointed toward the glass-strewn living room. Christine and Melinda were wrapped in each other's arms on the floor. He knelt down beside Christine and said her name again. His own pulse was pounding as he reached to check for hers.

She swatted his hand away, and the motion drew a moan that was music to his ears. "Whoa, take it easy," he cautioned as she unwrapped herself from Melinda and tried to sit up. Melinda scooted away and ran to Henry.

Christine tried to sit up, leaning on her arm to balance herself, and immediately let out a gasp of pain. Blood trickled from her cheek, but a quick inspection assured Blake it was a scratch from glass, not a bullet.

"Did they hit you?" He didn't see any sign of a gunshot wound, but he was taking no chances.

She shook her head weakly. "No. Thanks to you, we had time to get flat on the carpet. What happened?"

"The truck that we thought was tailing us earlier suddenly appeared on the street as I was leaving. I just had a bad feeling."

She offered a quick prayer of thanks. Tremors shook her body, and tears shimmered in her eyes. "They were trying to kill me, Blake." She shuddered hard. "If you hadn't waited, if you hadn't…" Tears overflowed and joined the trail of blood down her cheek. She slumped listlessly against a bullet-riddled chair, and his heart broke at the sight of her defeated expression.

He cast a glance over his shoulder at Henry, who was holding Melinda, both of them clearly still in shock. "Your alarm probably alerted the police, but you need to call 911 in case they return." He doubted that would happen today, but it was impossible for anyone to deny these men were not giving up. Henry had to realize that now.

Blake turned his attention back to Christine. "What hurts?"

She cradled her arm, the same one that had taken the brunt of yesterday's fall. "I think it's just my wrist. I was almost flat when they opened fire, but I landed hard on top of my arm, and my wrist bent." Her voice broke.

Blake sank down beside her and wrapped his arm around her. "You're okay, you're safe."

"Only because of you. What if you hadn't waited?" She looked up at him, her green eyes brimming with a mix of terror and pain.

"Shh." He placed a gentle finger on her lips. "Don't go there. I stayed because some instinct told me you needed me."

She swallowed hard, and he could see her struggling to regain her composure.

"Okay." She swallowed again. "Okay. I'm sorry. I don't usually fall apart like this." Her face flushed with growing embarrassment.

"You've got all the reason in the world to fall apart. You've witnessed a killing, been shot at three times now, suffered an injured shoulder and wrist and all man-

ner of cuts and bruises." He shook his head. "Honestly,
I'd be more worried if you didn't break down."

She nestled into his arms. "Oh, Blake. What have I
gotten into?"

Blake swallowed his own fear and just held her close.
Whatever she had witnessed must have been extremely
serious to cause this kind of reaction. And to his mind,
there was only one explanation—someone with power
needed something covered up. That was the only justification he could think of for this intense an effort to
kill her. The thought terrified him even more than the
feel of her snuggled against his side. She fit too well
for comfort.

Which was a good reason to move, but he didn't
want to.

The next few hours passed in a blur of police, crime
scene techs, interviews, phone calls and more interviews. Emergency technicians checked everyone over
and wrapped Christine's wrist. The detective, who had
been irritated by Blake's presence in the morning, gave
him full attention tonight as they hashed over the events
as Blake had witnessed them.

Outside television crews turned night into day as
their cameras lit up the sky. Blake could see reporters
interviewing neighbors and imagined all the "never
before in my neighborhood" comments that were
surely being uttered. Except it had happened in their
neighborhood—twice in one day.

The cameras also lit fear in Blake's heart. If someone
had been motivated to silence Christine before, the ante
had been seriously raised with the arrival of the news
crews. Hopefully, all the press attention would yield

information about the crime, but the more likely result was that the attempts to silence her would escalate.

Henry and Melinda chose to go stay with friends for as long as their house remained a crime scene. They wanted Christine to come with them, but Blake put his foot down. The one positive outcome of tonight was that the attack made it easy to convince his superiors to authorize a safe house for Christine. She would get all the protection she needed—from the Texas Rangers.

SEVEN

The aroma of coffee teased Christine awake, though it took a moment to adjust to her surroundings. She must have fallen asleep on the sofa. A vague recollection of Blake pulling a blanket over her and brushing her hair back with a gentle touch warmed her heart. She sighed, stretched and shook off the tender feelings.

It would be too easy to get attached to the handsome and kind Ranger. He and Dylan had been so good to her. The last three days she had spent here would have been the happiest she'd been in years if not for the fact that someone still wanted her dead.

It was a credit to Blake and the Rangers that there had been no more attempts on her life. The safe house, deep in Hill Country, was living up to its name. Unfortunately, there had been no progress toward solving the case, either. They had no more idea who the murder victim was than she'd had when she saw him die. Without his identity, figuring out who had killed him, and thus was after her, was feeling impossible. That fueled her frustration.

As peaceful as these past days had been, she couldn't go on like this. She couldn't live the rest of her life in hiding.

She also had the nagging feeling that she was missing something. She replayed the scene in her head again. Every terrifying detail unspooled through her mind in vivid color. She closed her eyes and tried to slow down the mental video. *There.* She had a sudden memory of something, a scrap of paper, slipping from the man's fingers as he fell. Was it a clue? Her heart raced in excitement. She needed a way to get back in that building to find out.

Her spirits sank just as quickly as they had surged. There was no way Blake would let her leave this house to investigate.

A knock on the open door interrupted her musings, and a blush heated her cheeks as she looked up to see Blake standing there bearing a steaming mug of coffee.

In another life, she would have been attracted to Blake. Scratch that. She definitely was attracted to him. She just couldn't allow anything to come of it. There was no place in her life right now for a relationship, no matter how strong, caring and gorgeous the Ranger was.

"Hello," she managed.

"Good morning, sleepyhead."

She rolled to her side and focused on the cup he handed her because she didn't think she could keep her thoughts from showing in her eyes. Despite all her protests, this was an awfully nice way to wake up.

She took a sip of her coffee and looked at the display on the wall clock—5:30 a.m.

"Someone's alert for this early," she teased, struggling for composure. "Good morning, Blake."

"In all fairness, I got a call that woke me." He paused until she looked up. "They found a body."

"What?" His words blew off the remaining embarrassment, and she bolted upright, sloshing coffee everywhere. "When? Where?" She took a breath. "How?"

"In a dumpster behind the building. Supposedly someone called in a tip."

She took a gulp of the remaining coffee and set the mug on the table. "Let's go."

"I don't want you to come with me—"

"I'm going," she insisted.

She caught herself and sank back against the sofa. "I don't mean to sound crazy enthusiastic, but you must know what it means to me that they found him." She rubbed eyes that had grown suspiciously moist. "Maybe now he can be identified, his family notified. Maybe now they'll start looking for his killer."

"I know." Blake leveled his gaze at her. "What I was starting to say is that I don't want you to come, but I don't want to leave you here alone either. I could drop you at Dylan's ranch."

She glared at him.

"It's been five days. I don't have to tell you what shape the body will be in."

She swallowed hard. "Honestly, I hadn't thought of that. But it's not enough to stay away." She paused a moment. "I appreciate you wanting to shield me, but I need to do this, Blake. And don't tell me it's too dangerous. The site will be swarming with police."

He sighed dramatically. "I figured that would be your reaction. How long do you need to get ready?"

She looked down at the now-coffee-splattered clothes she'd slept in. "Five minutes to wash up and change."

"Do you have ID?"

"In my wallet. Blake, do you know anything more?"

He shook his head. "No, I got a call from a friend, but he didn't have details."

Christine's mind raced as they drove downtown, but she kept silent trying to juggle conflicting emotions. On one level, the discovery of the body meant people would stop judging her sanity. She wouldn't be the assistant US attorney forced to take leave for imagining she witnessed a murder. She'd be able to get back to her caseload, back to the victims who needed her to stand up for them in court.

On another level, finding the body destroyed any fragment of hope that the man she'd seen hadn't been dead. The thought hit her like a bale of hay. She hadn't even realized until now that a corner of her brain had been holding out hope that she'd been wrong, that the man she'd seen get shot had actually not been dead and had been able to escape.

And then there was his family. Last night she and Blake had discussed investigating missing persons reports. Now a family would be notified their loved one was gone. The finality of it struck her with the same force it always did. Grieving families needed justice. Since a body had been found, that process could begin. A search would be on for the perpetrators. Finally.

On a professional level, Blake understood why Christine needed to identify the body. On a personal level, he still wasn't sure it was a good idea. Christine had been through a lot. He didn't consider her a fragile person, but everyone had a breaking point, and she had to be approaching hers. "You okay over there?"

She flashed a sad smile and shrugged. "Yeah."

"Having second thoughts?"

"About coming with you? No. It's just reality hitting hard."

"We can stop for coffee, take some time."

"No, let's just get this done."

Blake pulled up to the building and Christine commented on how different everything looked. She was right. The desolate block was now full of police cars, fire engines, ambulances and lots of onlookers, despite the early hour.

As Blake exited the car, he pulled out his Ranger badge. "Stay close," he whispered, taking her hand.

He approached the uniformed officer and flashed the badge. "Texas Ranger. I'm bringing in the assistant US attorney as witness."

He didn't give the man a chance to stop them as he continued past the barricades.

He repeated the maneuver as they rounded the building.

Christine had made it this far. He wasn't going to let anyone deny her the chance to identify the man she'd seen murdered.

He pushed his way through the crowd, holding her tightly beside him, until they reached the detective standing by the body.

He read the name off the badge and introduced himself. "I have Assistant US Attorney Christine Davis with me. She was a witness to the murder and would like to ID the body."

As he spoke, Christine pulled away and walked around the detective to where the medical examiner was at work.

"Hey, you can't go there."

Christine held up one hand and flashed her federal ID with the other. "I won't touch anything. I just—"

She crouched down next to the ME for barely a minute before the detective pulled her away. It was long enough.

Blake felt the tension radiating off her, felt her reaction before she gathered the words to speak. He put an arm around her shoulder and whispered in her ear. "Don't say anything."

"It's not him," she whispered back.

"I know. I got that from your reaction." He eyed the crowd that had gathered, wondering if the killers were in the crowd. Had they come to see the attraction? Or was this a setup?

Blake let his gaze roam the crowd, searching facial reactions. Most people appeared to be just curious bystanders. Those reactions he dismissed for the time being. There were other, more interesting people who drew his attention.

Dylan had done some research on the building's owners, and Blake recognized the man walking toward him from some photos Dylan had sent him. Ned Rivera was an influential real estate developer, and he looked seriously annoyed at the moment. Two of the cops stepped up to speak with Rivera, so Blake made a mental note to have his source check their backgrounds. Another man burst onto the scene with all the loudmouthed bravado Blake expected based on his reputation. He must be Rivera's rancher brother.

"What is going on here?"

Blake stood immobile as the older brother laid a restraining arm on his sibling.

"Calm down, Zeke. Remember the woman who

claimed she saw a man killed in our building? Apparently she was right. A tip led the police to this dumpster."

Rivera's voice was almost alarmingly calm. This was a man who was used to getting what he wanted, and he was setting up the scene as nothing more than a tragic inconvenience to be tolerated. The younger man had less self-control. He shrugged off his brother's arm and looked toward the dumpster and the body. "Not the first time a bum was found squatting here. Probably rival squatters got him. I told you we needed to clear out of this part of town."

Blake paid close attention to the carefully controlled tension that built in the older brother. "That's not the issue now," he drawled. "Someone died, and these good officers are going to see justice done regardless of his social status."

Blake could feel the oil rolling off the man. He almost preferred the angry rancher who was shrugging off the detective's attempts to move him behind the barricade. Apparently, both brothers were used to having their way. He needed to ask Christine if their voices sounded familiar.

He turned to check with her, but she was no longer at his side. Where had she gone? He'd been concentrating so much on watching the interaction of the players that he hadn't been paying attention to her.

Unease curled in his chest. Some protector he was. It wasn't likely she'd come to harm with all the law enforcement officers hovering around, but still... She was his responsibility. He scanned the scene with growing impatience until he noticed a door slightly ajar and knew exactly where she'd gone. She'd been dying for a chance to get back in that building, and now it had been handed to her.

Blake eased away, making sure not to draw attention to his actions as he headed into the building after her. Once inside, he realized he had no idea where to go.

He stood for a moment, trying to orient himself in relation to where she had burst out of the building and run in front of him. He'd go there and work backward if necessary. Heading deeper into the building, he whispered her name, but there was no response.

He went a little farther, raised his voice a bit more. "Christine. Where are you?"

EIGHT

Christine heard the footsteps following her into the building. Why was someone else even in the building? Was this a trap? Sweat dotted her brow and chills raced down her arms. Her chest grew tight as panic overwhelmed her. She should have waited for Blake. She should have stayed outside where she was safe.

Too late now, she reprimanded herself. *Lord, help me, calm me, be my rock. Help me know what to do.* Instinct made her keep moving forward. She had the advantage of knowing where she was headed, although if the killer was following, he'd know that was her probable goal. She scurried sideways, trying to keep behind the construction debris.

"Christine, where are you?"

Christine sank to the floor, relief pouring through her as she recognized Blake's voice. She couldn't answer. What if someone overheard them? Maybe it had been no mistake the door had been left open. Given all the attempts on her life recently, it seemed a real possibility. She had to get to him and warn him. Forcing her legs to support her, she circled back around and came up beside him. "I'm right here."

"What were you thinking coming in here?"

His harsh whisper stung. She hung her head. "It was stupid, I know. But I saw the door open and knew I had to take the chance."

He wrapped his arms tightly around her. "I couldn't find you."

For the second time in the last few minutes, Christine's breath was trapped in her lungs, only this time it was from the reassurance of his arms around her and the comforting tension of being held so close. His arms were so strong, and they held her so securely that in a way it felt like he was holding her together. She burrowed into his embrace and let the tension and fear seep away.

"Did I frighten you?"

She nodded against his chest. "It was my own fault. I shouldn't have come in. So when I heard footsteps, I had a flashback." She shuddered. "It triggered a panic attack."

His hand smoothed over her hair. "Understandable," he murmured.

Maybe to him. She was getting tired of her reactions. She had to find a way past this recurring fear. She had to find a way to make a life again.

Fearing he would make her leave if she seemed too scared, Christine pulled back and looked up into his eyes, ready to reassure him. The unexpected intensity in his gaze stole her breath. There was something in his eyes that calmed and confused her at the same time. His face hovered just above hers, and she felt him drawing her in. Her gaze dropped to his lips, and tremors that had nothing to do with fear shivered through her.

She dragged her gaze away. She was not here for

kissing, and she was not blowing this opportunity on a romance that had no future.

"Come." Her voice cracked, so she tugged his arm. "I didn't have a chance to tell you earlier, but I remembered something this morning. The man was holding a piece of paper and he dropped it when he fell. When I saw the door open, I knew I had to come see if I could find it."

She knew Blake's head must be spinning with her sudden reversal from panic to determined, but he followed right behind as she wove her way around piles of debris. "I'm a bit turned around coming from the back, but I figured I could best orient myself if I crossed to where I came in," she explained in a whisper as she walked. "The body was found in the alley behind the building, but the open door was on the side, so walking at a diagonal should bring us to the right place." She stopped and pointed. "I think I was over there when I saw him."

Her eyes shone as she gained her bearings. "That's the doorway I came through." She narrated softly as she traced her path. "I walked this way, and I was right over here when I first heard the voices. It was too late to back out, so I hid in an alcove over here."

She crossed to where she'd hidden. "There was a drop cloth here, but it's gone now." She chewed on her lip as she considered it. "Do you think they wrapped the body in that?"

Blake nodded. "It would explain why there was no blood trail, but there should be some evidence where he fell unless he was on the drop cloth."

The last thing Christine wanted to do was relive the scene again, but if that was what it took to solve the crime, she could force the memory.

"I had my back against this wall when he burst through. He reached out, but his hand didn't come close to touching mine. As I said, he had a piece of paper in his hand. He was trying to hand it to me, and then he fell. I didn't see where it went." She took out her phone and switched on the flashlight. "Help me look. Maybe it's still here."

"You realize we're probably trampling all over a crime scene," Blake reminded her.

Her prosecutorial instincts cringed at the thought. "Ostensibly, the police have already been through here and found nothing."

Blake glanced over his shoulder. "I don't think anyone noticed we left, or else they just didn't figure we'd come in here, but we need to hurry."

"Okay, but give me a minute. Something feels off, even if I'm not getting what it is."

Christine paced back and forth. "This is going to be the second pair of shoes I've ruined in here," she murmured. "The first ones were covered with blood, and these are getting coated in mud. Wait. Mud." She looked down at her boots. The soles were caked in a sandy mud.

"Blake, that's what's off. There was no mud in here. I looked down and saw bloody footprints on concrete. Not dirt or sand. Solid concrete. That's why there are no bloodstains. They covered them over with dirt and loose cement. That's why it's sticking to my shoes."

"Okay, watch where you're standing. I'll call for someone from the Rangers to come in and check it out."

He stepped aside to make the call and Christine stood there kicking her toe around in the dirt and cement mixture as she tried to listen to what he was saying. Someone on the other end of the phone must have been arguing with him. She heard him say something about jurisdiction before his angry voice merged with the memories flooding her mind. The angry men were coming closer.

Did she see you?

I don't know.

We can't take a chance. Find her.

She started to back away. She had to get out of here.

"Christine, stop."

How did he know her name? How did they know who she was? It didn't matter if she broke free, they'd keep coming after her.

"Christine, it's me, Blake. You're safe."

She shook herself.

Blake stood in front of her, hands in the air in sur-render mode, a concerned look on his face.

Blake. She took a deep breath and sagged back against an exposed stud. "I'm sorry. Your angry voice, it caused another flashback." She sucked in a deep breath. "Just give me a minute. I'll be fine."

Blake's phone vibrated, and he turned away to an-swer it. Christine slid down along the door frame. She was going to need more than a minute. She buried her head in her hands and tried to breathe through it, des-perate to compose herself. When she finally felt she had herself under control, she looked up to see Blake talking animatedly on the phone.

This was a disaster. She should have known better than to come back in here. She was reliving every pan-icked moment. And for what? This wouldn't change anything for the better, and it might make things worse. Would she lose her job? Be disbarred for interfering with a crime scene. She laughed out loud. They couldn't have it both ways. Couldn't tell her she imagined it and then punish her for interfering.

Blake looked over at her when she laughed, and she lowered her gaze. What was he thinking? Minutes ago she'd been in his arms, and now he probably thought she was losing what was left of her mind. She turned away, and that was when she saw the scrap of paper.

It flashed in her mind again, the man's arm extended, the paper flitting through his fingers.

She hesitated for just a second. "Blake," she whispered, and beckoned to him. "Look. I found it."

He raised his hand to signal to her to wait while he finished the call.

Tempted as she was to grab the paper, professional ethics held firm. She couldn't bring herself to remove it from the crime scene, so she snapped a photo with her phone, instead. She didn't see anything written on it. She searched the floor until she found a nail she could use to flip it and snapped a photo of the back.

"Do you smell something?"

Blake's voice startled her, and she sniffed the air. "Gas?"

"I think. Let's go."

The faint smell quickly grew to overpowering. Fear caught in her belly. Something was definitely wrong. "What's happening?"

"I think this was a setup. Someone had to have opened a gas line. No leak would build that quickly." Blake grasped her hand. "We have to get out of here fast."

In that instant, Christine realized the depth of her mistake. That door hadn't been left open accidentally. It had been meant to lure her into the building. So they could finally kill her.

She shivered against the dizziness as gas fumes filled her lungs. Her eyes burned and breathing became more difficult. The room started to spin on her.

She pulled off her sweater and wrapped it around her face. Blake did the same with his jacket and grabbed her hand again. *This way*, he motioned, leading her deeper into the building. "The air feels a little clearer here. I'm sure they expected us to run for the door we came in. It's probably locked by now."

"They want us to die in here."

Blake hugged her to him. "Well, we just won't give them what they want."

He turned left, but Christine flashed back to the first time she'd tried to escape this building. She tugged on his hand. "No, this way. I know the way out."

At least she thought she did. So much had changed in here in the past few days. Obviously someone was committed to removing all possible evidence. Relying purely on instinct, she quickly wove her way through the maze of construction debris knowing that time was not in their favor. The gas fumes seemed to be spreading this way. They had to get out before they were overcome.

Where was the window? She turned in circles, disoriented by the combination of fumes and changes.

"I don't get it. There was a window right here." She pointed at a wall. She was sure that's where the window had been.

Blake pulled her toward the wall. "It was the window, but it's been boarded over."

The smell of gas grew stronger. They were trapped. Fear swamped Christine. This attack had been coordinated with the precision of a military campaign, every contingency planned for.

She was overcome with an urge to sink to the ground and give in. It was all too much. They were going to win. She didn't have the breath to fight.

"Come on, Christine." Blake shook her. "We'll get out, but I need you to help."

He'd found the hammer that must have been used to board over the window. Wielding the claw end, he began to pry the board loose.

A whooshing sound started behind them. They were running out of time.

"Blake, it's going to blow."

She couldn't believe she was going to die here today after surviving being shot at in this very same building. Why hadn't she listened to Henry and backed off?

Because she was her mother's daughter and had a legacy to fulfill, which meant she couldn't give up, could not let them win. She pulled herself to her feet, wobbling a little at the wooziness, and leaned against the wall. Spying a pile of a metal pipes, Christine grabbed one and staggered toward Blake. He was obviously fighting against the symptoms from the gas, but was still working on the board, so she slid her metal under the plywood and put all her strength into leveraging it. She could feel the wood begin to pull loose.

"That does it, Chris. Keep pulling."

The sound of explosions behind them gave her all the impetus she needed. Together they pulled the plywood off the frame.

"Duck," Blake yelled. Hard on the heels of his words, a fireball shot through the room, igniting any flammable surface it touched. He threw himself over her as they were instantly surrounded by an inferno.

NINE

They hadn't come this close to escape just to burn to death.

Blake used his body to shield Christine as he searched for cover. He spied some tarps scattered on the floor. They must have been treated with a flame retardant because they were the only things not on fire. He rolled sideways so he could quickly grab them, then rolled back to her side. "Here, wrap this around yourself."

Her movements were slow, dulled by fumes and heat, and she didn't respond. She was coughing, but barely moving otherwise. He had no choice except to carry her.

Pulling the tarp closely around his head, he swaddled her like a mummy and lifted her into a fireman's carry, then charged through the flames toward the opening.

Once he was clear, Blake pushed the cloth away from their faces. All of the attention was focused on the other side of the building, where the body had been found. Sirens sounded, lights flashed. No one paid any attention as Blake raced along the north side of the building. Once he reached the far corner, he dashed across the street and ducked behind another building. He gently lowered Christine to the ground and unwrapped the heavy material. "Breathe," he ordered.

She bent over, sucking in clean air as coughs choked her. He pounded her back. "That's it. Cough it up. Breathe in clean air through your nose."

He watched, deeply concerned, as she struggled, but she followed his directions. Color slowly returned to her face.

"We can't stay here," he warned, his gaze darting from her face to the burning building. "I think it's going to collapse and we need to be far away. Can you run on your own or do you need me to carry you?"

She just nodded, saving breath as she started off in a slow jog. Blake grasped her hand again, coaxing her to move faster.

They'd barely made it a block before a thunderous roar indicated the building was imploding. The force of the collapse knocked them off their feet.

A hush filled the air as clouds of dust and debris swept over them. Blake pulled Christine into his chest and wrapped his jacket around her head as they huddled together. He lowered his own head, burying his face in her hair. He stroked his hand over her back and whispered assurances.

Long minutes passed before it felt safe to lift their heads. Christine stood and gingerly began dusting herself off. She took in the devastation around them, and Blake caught the moment it really hit her how close they'd come to dying. She started to shake uncontrollably. He reached for her again and pulled her into his arms, then guided her to a doorway.

They huddled in the doorway, listening to sirens wail as emergency crews responded to the explosion. Little by little her shudders subsided.

Blake was worried. "I should take you to a hospital."

She shook her head. "We'd be sitting ducks." She coughed. "The one thing we have going for us is that they think we were in the building." Christine looked at the plume of smoke and shuddered. "If they think we died in there, it might buy us some time."

Blake wanted to kick himself for putting her in danger. "I feel incredibly stupid for falling into their trap. I should have recognized it as one the minute you knew it was the wrong body."

Christine cleared her throat and hung her head. "Don't blame yourself. I'm the one who snuck away and went into the building. If I hadn't done that, you wouldn't have followed, and we'd both have been safe."

He gazed down at her and shook his head. "What a pair we are."

She dazzled him with her return smile. "But we're alive." Her smile faded. "Oh, no. Your truck."

He made a face and shrugged. "I imagine it's toast."

Christine buried her face in her hands. "I hope no one was hurt in the explosion."

Blake tilted her chin up. "Breathe deeply. You need oxygen. I imagine they cleared the area as soon as they smelled gas."

Her coughing had subsided and she was looking better. "Do you think you can walk? We need to get away from here."

She looked up and smiled again. "I just realized something. My car is still in the lot from the other day. The ambulance took me right to the hospital and, honestly, I've been so preoccupied I forgot it was there."

"Where is the lot?"

She stood and tried to get her bearings, but her head still felt muddled. "I was walking in front of the building, but I still had several blocks to go, so it should be over that way."

Blake looked in the direction she pointed, then pulled up a map on his phone. "If we go down two blocks and work our way across, we should be able to get to your car without anyone noticing. Do you have keys?"

Christine opened the purse she'd carried across her chest. "Yep. Right here." She tossed them to him. "Is your head clear enough to drive? I wouldn't want to risk it yet."

"Yes, and it's getting better as we walk. I think we got away from the intense gas fast enough to avoid any lingering exposure dangers."

Fifteen minutes of circling around brought them to the lot. Blake beeped the unlock button, and he and Christine climbed into the car. She closed her eyes and leaned her head back against the seat.

"Are you sure you don't need to go to the ER?"

She shook her head. "No, I already feel better."

"Then what's wrong?"

She opened her eyes and faced him. "I was just thinking that I won't blame you if you want to give up."

Blake offered her a small smile. "The words *give up* are not in a Texas Ranger's vocabulary."

"It's not your fight."

What was she doing? It may not have started as his fight, but there was no conceivable way he was going to abandon her.

Her face was cast downward now, so he took her hands in his and lifted them so she looked up again. "Christine, if this is too much for you, we can turn it over to the Rangers completely. I can try to get witness protection for you."

She shook her head. "I was trying to talk you out of

it for your own safety. I'm not giving up. Everything they are doing is just proving to me that I'm right. That I did see exactly what I said I saw. I might have made a mistake going into that warehouse today, but they made a bigger one."

"How so?"

"Trying to trap me in there, blowing up the warehouse—they just strengthened my resolve. They went to a lot of trouble to try to kill me. No one does that to disprove an imaginary killing."

She closed her eyes and sank back against the seat. "I'm just sorry for your sake that I dragged you into it."

Blake didn't know whether to laugh or be angry. He started the car instead, headed out of the parking lot and in the opposite direction from the building collapse.

"His eyes were the wrong color."

"What?"

"The body they found. His eyes were open." She shuddered. "I have a vision imprinted in my head of the victim coming toward me after he was shot the first time. He had his hand extended. He was looking right at me, his eyes begging for help. They were blue. Startling bright blue. The man in the dumpster had dark eyes. He was also a lot older."

Blake stayed silent, letting her get out the thoughts rumbling through her brain.

"Also, I'm not a medical examiner obviously, but this guy didn't smell like he'd been dead for very long. I could smell cigarettes on him. Did you pick up on that?"

Blake grinned. "I can see why you're such a good prosecutor. You're focusing on all the key elements."

Christine turned and stared out the window. Focusing on small details was her specialty. Right now it was also a coping mechanism. No matter what Blake said, she felt guilty. He'd come within a hair's breadth of losing his life today because he was trying to help her. And she didn't even want to think what the bad guys might try next, once they found out the gas hadn't killed her.

But what would she do without him? She might have confirmation that she'd really witnessed a murder, yet she was no closer to determining who the victim had been. The paper! In the rush to escape, she'd completely forgotten about the scrap of paper. She opened her phone and studied her photos. The first one was blank, as she'd noticed, but the flip side had writing on it. Excitement pulsed as she zoomed in on the words.

"What aren't you telling me?" Blake glanced over at her as he pulled up to a stoplight.

"Hmm? What are you talking about?"

"There's something you're not telling me."

Christine turned and stared out the window.

"You'll think I've lost it," she whispered.

He laughed. "After everything we've been through this week, I'm not sure anything you say could make me think that."

Knowing she had to trust him, Christine turned back to face him. "I think the guy I saw murdered was Amish."

Blake's eyes widened, but nothing in his demeanor questioned her sanity.

"Explain."

"I'll try, but it's more a feeling. A combination of things. Remember, right before the gas started leaking I said I'd found a paper on the floor?" She held out her phone and showed him the photo of a crumpled scrap of brown paper. It looked like it had been part of a bag. "It has the address of the building written on it."

"Okay."

"It also says Texas Country Amish General Store."

"There are Amish in Texas?"

"See, that's why I figured you'd think I was off."

"Look it up."

Christine grinned. "One step ahead of you." She was already typing "Amish in Texas" into her search. An Amish settlement in Bee County came up, along with a list of Amish settlements that had begun and failed. She was about to surrender to the idea she was wrong, when an article title caught her eye. "Apparently, there's one community down in Bee County, and another one…"

Her voice trailed off as she typed the name of the general store into her phone and hit Search.

"Blake, it's real. There's an Amish settlement in New Grange. I know where that is. Melinda has a family ranch down in that area. I spent summers there as a teen."

She quickly scanned the article. "It says the founders of this settlement came to help out after Hurricane Ike and decided to stay."

Excitement bubbled. "Listen to this," she read. "A notice in their local newsletter brought Amish youth to Texas in the wake of Hurricane Ike. Eager to serve, these young men and women traveled from Indiana to help rescue herds of cattle stranded in the aftermath of the hurricane. They built fences so the ranchers could put their cows back."

Blake interrupted. "Okay. That sounds great, but Hurricane Ike was a long time ago. What does that have to do with this case?"

"I don't know, but it has to be connected." She turned

back to the search engine and got more specific. A sense of anticipation gripped her now. Until she'd read those words, she hadn't realized just how much she was counting on this clue.

"Just because the man had a bag from an Amish store doesn't make him Amish. Maybe he was a tourist in the wrong place at the wrong time."

Christine chewed on her lip as she mulled over that possibility.

"No, I heard them arguing. The voices definitely sounded like they knew each other." She shivered. "I remember the man who shot him saying, 'That'll teach you to cross me.'"

"That still doesn't mean he's Amish. Why do you think that?"

Christine closed her eyes and tried to remember. "There was something about the way he was dressed. Not like your typical Texan. He was wearing dark pants and a white shirt."

Blake coughed to get her attention and pointed to himself. Underneath the dirt and debris from the explosion, he was wearing the same colors.

"Point taken, but he wasn't wearing a tie or a badge." Her head jerked up. "He was wearing suspenders."

Blake laughed. "I'll give you that then. He doesn't sound like your average Texan."

"Blake, I want to go there."

He sighed and shook his head. "Figured as much. You sure it's not the aftereffects of breathing too much gas?"

"No, seriously. We have to go down there. Well, I have to. You don't have to come. This is the first serious lead I've had. The first chance that someone may have information to prove I'm…right."

TEN

Blake heard the pause before she added "right" and knew that hadn't been her original choice of word. She didn't have any way of knowing, but he totally understood what it felt like to have your mental health challenged in a way that suggested you weren't capable of doing your job. If he was honest, part of his willingness to take on this assignment had been his need to prove he was healed. An internal investigation had cleared him of any wrongdoing in Sofia's case, but that didn't mean he'd ever get over losing someone he'd promised to protect.

"I should take you to the safe house and go down myself."

"Oh, no you don't," Christine shot back. "This is my lead."

"I don't care whose lead it is. I need to keep you safe. So far, that has proven to be the only place we can do that."

"You're forgetting something."

Blake heard the intransigence in her voice. This was going to be a battle. "What?"

"As far as they know, we were in that building. How

much safer can I be than them thinking I'm already dead?"

Grief shuddered through Blake at her words. He'd been avoiding facing how close a line they'd walked with eternity this morning. Still, she had a point. And the alternative of leaving her alone at the safe house didn't really appeal.

He tossed her his phone. "Plug it into the GPS."

She did as requested and then settled into her corner. "Will you be offended if I take a nap?" She yawned. "It's all catching up with me."

She was out before he could even answer. Blake flexed his shoulders and settled in for the drive. He wasn't looking forward to the time alone with his thoughts.

Last night, Dylan had stopped by the safe house. After Christine had fallen asleep on the sofa, the brothers had a long conversation about a variety of topics ranging from their childhood to their recent cases. Inevitably the conversation had turned to his last case, the one that had resulted in Sofia's death. Dylan posed a disturbing question, and it echoed in Blake's brain now. *Was he trying to find redemption for losing Sofia by saving Christine?*

Possibly? Maybe even likely?

Sofia was a woman who had been in his protective custody while they worked to take down her abusive husband for drug trafficking. In the end, she hadn't been able to turn on him, and she'd ended up dead at his hands. Blake blamed himself for not seeing that coming. It was something he would never get over. But to Dylan's point, why was that relevant now if he'd submerged the guilt and used the motivation to provide the safety and investigative power Christine needed?

Or was that just his own conscience trying to justify his actions?

None of his questions would be answered now, so he shoved them back down. Better that he focus on the current case and the possible lead they'd found. Amish. He hadn't seen that coming, either.

When GPS announced they were approaching the town, he decided to rouse his sleepy partner. "Christine?" He spoke softly, not wanting to startle her.

She didn't respond. He tried again, a little louder, and she still didn't open her eyes. He could hardly blame her for sleeping so deeply. They'd nearly died this morning. How close they'd come rattled him, and he was used to facing danger as part of his job. It wasn't supposed to be part of hers.

Seeing a sign for fuel and coffee up ahead, Blake waited until he could pull into the parking lot. After unlatching his seat belt, he leaned toward her, brushed the hair from her forehead and gently squeezed her shoulder. "Come on, sleepyhead. Time to wake up."

"Blake?" Her brilliant green eyes shot open, but they were dazed and confused. She reached up and rubbed them. "Where are we?"

Blake swallowed the emotion that threatened to swamp him. "About a mile from New Grange. I thought maybe you could use some coffee."

A huge smile wreathed her face. "Could I ever."

"Don't get your hopes up. It's just roadside coffee."

She rolled her shoulders and stretched. "Nothing cream and sugar can't fix."

"Do you want to wait here or come in?"

He could hear the effect of the morning in her reply. "I'll come with you."

Once they were back in the car, Blake pointed out their location on the GPS map. "I've been seeing signs for the town for the past twenty miles. Seems like it's quite the tourist destination."

"Seriously? How did we not know about this? I guess it makes sense if the families only settled here after Ike. By then I was in law school, so I wasn't really coming down here at all."

Blake slowed as they approached a curve in the road. Traffic signs warning drivers to slow down bore images of buggies.

Christine leaned forward. Fields spread out before them as they came around the curve, and in the distance he could see what must be the center of the settlement. Houses lined a single road that led into a central circle. Fields spread out like sectors on a clock.

"Oh, Blake. It's sweet. I didn't expect this at all. Well, not that I really knew what to expect, but I didn't expect it would look so successful. I guess that's the word. After reading about all the settlements that failed, I didn't expect much."

"They do appear prosperous." Which immediately set his radar on alert, a hazard of his job. "Tourism must be profitable."

Blake followed signs to a parking lot where they were to leave the car and be ferried into the main part of town in a buggy. Christine was delighted, so he kept his questions to himself. She deserved some fun.

Their driver introduced himself as Moses and offered her a pamphlet detailing the shops. Christine read the list aloud. "There's the General Store, of course, and a quilt shop, and a furniture store where you can take wood carving lessons."

"Sorry, no wood carving lessons today," their driver interrupted. "Samuel is away, so the shop is closed up."

Christine nudged Blake and mouthed, *Away?* Her face fell, and her enthusiasm dimmed as she considered what that might mean.

Blake tried to cheer her up. Just so she didn't give anything away, he assured himself. "I see there's a restaurant. You must be starving by now."

"Oh, you'll want to visit there for certain sure."

"Let's start there then," Blake suggested. "Breakfast seems a lifetime ago." He winced at his own words, but Christine just gave him a wry smile. He knew she was thinking a restaurant would give them the perfect opportunity to ask questions. He needed to caution her not to be too obvious. This wasn't a witness stand.

They entered the restaurant under a sign that proclaimed *Wilkum*. The interior was simple but appeared comfortable and friendly. A few guests lingered around large wooden tables where food was being served family style.

A young woman in traditional Amish garb greeted them. "*Guder daag.* You are here in between our main meal times, but you are hungry, yes?"

Blake smiled at her. "We're famished. Anything you can give us would be most appreciated."

The young woman smiled back. "There is always food here." She led them to a smaller table in the back near a window. "Mamm will come tell you about our menu in a few moments."

Christine and Blake settled in at the table, and she gazed around the room. "This is wonderful."

"I am so pleased you like our restaurant." An older woman, who introduced herself as Mrs. Byler, approached, her smile equally warm and welcoming. "My *dochder* said you are very hungry. You could have a late breakfast, but since it is almost time for lunch, I suggest our Thresher's dinner. You will start with ham-and-bean soup, followed by slices of country chicken or beef and egg noodles. Then, of course, dessert. Grossmammi's grape pie is today's special."

Blake could see Christine was itching to interview the woman, so he quickly intervened. "That sounds wonderful, doesn't it, Chris?"

Christine followed his lead. "It does. But it sure doesn't sound like any other Texas menu I've seen."

The woman chuckled. "It's not. Originally our people come from Indiana so our menu reflects our regional dishes. Variety is good, even for Texans. You can't live on tacos and brisket all the time."

Christine laughed. "That's almost exactly what I've been doing."

"Well then, you are ready for something completely different." She left them with the promise of returning to check on how they liked their meal.

"I guess we should have discussed how to approach this." Blake unfolded his napkin and took a sip of the coffee that had magically appeared. "So much better than gas station coffee."

"You don't have to worry." Christine sounded defensive. "I'm not going to ask her about the murder."

Blake softened and reached to take her hand. "I'm not saying you would. It's just been a long, stressful morning, and I don't think either of us really thought through what we'd do once we got here. Let's just enjoy our meal and see where this goes."

Christine acquiesced. "It will be nice to know I can eat and be completely safe." The unspoken *for now* echoed between them.

After they'd eaten their fill, Mrs. Byler brought them pie and coffee. She also pulled up a chair to visit. "What brings you to our settlement?"

Christine met Blake's gaze, and he could read her confusion. Did the woman know more than they thought?

"Tourism matters to us. I always like to know what brings people to us."

Christine let out a barely perceptible sigh of relief. "I recently learned about this community. I was surprised…and curious. I used to spend my summers down here, but I don't think you were here then. I hope saying I was curious doesn't sound disrespectful. I don't mean it that way. I'm genuinely interested in how you ended up here. What is it about this area? Why did you come?"

Mrs. Byler settled back in her chair. "That's both easy and hard to answer. Many of our young men and women came down to volunteer their services after Hurricane Ike." Her face softened. "For us the work was a blessing from *Gott*. Back home, the young people struggle. There is little work for them. There is not enough land for them to have their own farms. The factories don't have work like they used to.

"But Texas." She smiled. "My *maan*, my husband, he was like one of your early settlers. He saw such hope in Texas. He asked the bishop if we might come." She smiled at the memory. "He felt that being out here, away from pretty much everything was what *Gott* wanted from us. He loved this land, my *maan*. The wide-open spaces. He felt close to *Gott* here. He felt the work would keep the boys busy, away from temptation."

Her face fell briefly, and Blake saw Christine pick up on it.

"But?"

"Nothing. Life here has been *gut*."

"Your husband, he is gone?" Christine asked softly.

She sighed. "*Jah*. His heart was younger in spirit than health."

"Who runs the farms now?"

The smile faltered again. "It is more than just farms and not just my family. There are other families—fifteen of us in this settlement. Our men tried to learn from the failures of older settlements. We have many businesses. My son, Samuel, carves beautiful furniture. The girls sell quilts and baked goods. Then there is the restaurant." Her smile returned as she gestured to the room. "It fills our hearts to serve good food to those who visit us."

"Moses told us about your son's woodworking," Christine interjected. "He also mentioned Samuel was away. Will he be back soon? Blake hoped to see his work."

Again that cloud briefly crossed her face, but she quickly mustered her composure. "I do not know. Where are you from? Some of his work is sold in stores in San Antonio and Austin."

Christine managed to contain herself until they'd paid their bill and exited the restaurant, but as they left the building, she grabbed Blake's arm. "What can we do? There's a connection here. I feel it." Her shoulders sagged. "But I can't just suggest to a mother that maybe her son isn't home because he's dead."

"You can't, and you shouldn't. We don't know that yet, Christine. It could be complete coincidence."

"You go right on believing that," she retorted. "I don't want it to be true, Blake. I don't want this sweet family to suffer more loss. But so much fits."

He shook his head. "It fits because you want it to." He tilted his head to stop her protest. "I don't mean that you want him to be dead, but I know you need an answer. You need to know who the victim is. Let's not rush to conclusions. We haven't even visited the General Store yet. Let's do that with an open mind."

His attitude reminded her that this was work to him. He was a Texas Ranger used to investigating cases based on facts, not whims. And she knew better. She needed to remember to think like the prosecutor she was, and not a person who jumped to conclusions.

"All right. After that I want to visit the quilt shop." She gazed up at him somberly and grasped his hand as they waited to cross the street to the store. "I don't want her son to be dead, and I don't want to think any of these nice people are doing something illegal, but I will keep an open mind. I do know how to be impartial. My work depends on it."

He squeezed her hand. "I know you do." His expression softened. "I also know how hard this is on you. We've made a lot of progress today, but it's been a long day, so let's just gather what info we can, and we'll process it later."

Christine agreed. Had it been only this morning they'd gotten the call about the body? She had to be patient. They'd made more progress today than they had in all the other days combined. Blake was right. It was a lot to take in.

As they entered the General Store, she was gravely aware that this had been the name of the store on the scrap of paper the victim had held out to her. Was he Mrs. Byler's son, or just another tourist like them? Had he bought something here? Was that why he had the scrap of paper? Blake was right. She was making too many assumptions. She needed facts.

The store was charming, and Christine temporarily shoved her questions from her mind as she took in her surroundings. Barrels beside the counter contained dry goods. Shelves along one wall held large jars of preserved vegetables and smaller ones of various jams and jellies. She and Blake wandered through the aisles, filling a woven basket with assorted treats, and she kept her eyes open for any kind of clue.

The basket grew heavy, but their sleuthing turned up nothing. "Why don't you head to the quilt shop, and I'll deliver our packages to the car," Blake suggested. "I'll meet you outside the shop."

Much as she hated to admit defeat, Christine acknowledged there was nothing here that would help them—at least nothing she recognized. She headed down the street to the shop, hoping to find one of the quilting ladies ready to talk.

She knocked on the open door, and a young Amish woman standing beside a wall of quilts waved her in. Christine stepped through the doorway into a glorious world of color and craftsmanship. Quilts were everywhere, displayed along the walls and draped over furniture. A massive carved table held quilted bags, pot holders and place mats. Pillows tumbled in a corner. Handmade faceless dolls lined the staircase like a group of wallflowers waiting to join the party. In the center back of the store, a group of women sat around a quilting frame, laughing and chatting as they stitched. Their expressions were so welcoming as Christine approached that she yearned to pull up a chair and join them.

The quilt they were working on was a riot of color offset by intricate stitching. "This is stunning," she murmured.

"Danke," one of the older women replied.

The woman who had waved her in greeted her now. "I am Rebekah. Welcome to our shop. Is there something I can help you with, or would you like to look around?"

Christine smiled and gestured to the quilters. "I planned to look around, but I think I could just sit and watch them all day." A memory tickled at her mind. "My mother took me to a quilting bee when I was very little." She teased on the strands of thought. "My grandmother and her friends from church, I think. They were doing something for children in a hospital." Her smile broadened as memory flooded her senses. "I remember now. They would meet every Saturday morning and work on quilts for the infants. I secretly wished they would make one for me."

"Would you like to join us?"

"Oh, no. I don't want to ruin your beautiful work. May I sit and watch instead?"

"You are welcome to sit with us," Rebekah told her. "But there is no need for idle hands." She brought over a basket full of colorful pieces of cloth. "You can practice stitching these pieces together if you have time."

Christine glanced at her watch. Blake would be looking for her soon, but this was too good an opportunity to pass up. "I'd love to. Thank you. *Danke*," she added with a smile as she selected several strips in shades of blue. "My name is Christine. I'm from Austin."

The women continued to speak softly about this and that, babies and recipes, plans for the spring and summer, concerns for children.

"Do you have any *boppli*, Christine?"

A wave of intense longing swept over Christine at the question. For the first time in her life, she wished the answer was yes. Sitting here with these women, absorbing their peace and happiness in their family ties, made her want things she'd never dreamed of. If she was honest, a certain handsome Ranger was probably playing into it, as well. But there could be no future there.

"No. I'm not married." She shrugged. "My work keeps me busy."

"And what is that?"

"I'm a prosecutor. I work at putting bad guys behind bars."

"That is *gut* work," a woman who introduced herself as Sarah commented.

"It is fulfilling to help people. Cartels and trafficking ruin people's lives. I work to stop them." The nods and surreptitious glances emboldened her. "It must be rough being so close to the border. Do you have problems with them here or are they respectful of your ways?"

The expressions on the women's faces grew a bit wary, and their welcome felt a tad less certain. Christine continued, "We hear so much about problems down near the border. I was just wondering how you manage."

Sarah, who was clearly their leader, smiled sweetly

and said, "I can't even imagine why anyone would want to give us a hard time."

"You're saying you have no problems?"

"Not that anyone has discussed with me."

"That is good news then." They sewed in awkward silence for a few more minutes before Christine lifted the mess she'd made with the fabric. She sighed. "Aren't you relieved you didn't allow me to wreck your quilt?" She set the fabric aside and rose. "I think I'll just look around and buy something that someone far more talented created."

Rebekah rose with her. "It's not so bad, really. It just takes practice and patience."

"You are kind." Christine ran her hand along the carved wood table. "Did the local woodworker make this?"

Rebekah nodded. "My *bruder*, Samuel. He does *gut* work."

Good was an understatement. The table was extraordinary. "I heard his shop is closed. I would love to recommend his work to my friends. Do you know when it will open?"

There was that telltale look, the same fallen face and quick recovery as her mother had shown.

"I'm sorry, I do not know."

"Is your brother in trouble, Rebekah?"

The girl's gaze flew to her face. "Why would you say that?"

Christine glanced out the window and saw Blake waiting on the sidewalk. He would not be happy she'd asked the question.

"Christine, do you know my brother?"

"What?" Christine swung her head back around to

Rebekah. "No, I only asked because everyone seems so secretive about when his shop may reopen. I'm sorry to alarm you."

The girl's expression eased, but she still seemed guarded. Christine decided it was time to make an exit. She picked up a quilted tote bag. "My friend is waiting, so I'll just take this for now."

She waited while Rebekah packaged the bag and rang her up. Although something felt off and she wanted to pursue it, instinct said this was not the time. It was too soon to push. If the victim she'd seen murdered was Samuel, they obviously didn't know.

"Thank you so much for letting me share this time. I hope I'll be able to come back again." As Christine reached into her wallet for the money to pay, her fingers brushed across the pocket with her business cards. She slipped one out and handed it to Rebekah with the money. "As I said, I'm a lawyer. I can help if you have any problems."

By the time Christine stepped out, Blake had wandered off. She could see him up ahead squatting down and chatting with a little Amish girl. The child was speaking animatedly, gesturing at a trellis of vines. As Christine watched, Blake nodded and lifted the girl up so she could reach something. His head was tilted toward the child, and whatever he said sent her into peals of laughter.

Blake set the child on her feet, and she scampered off. He turned toward Christine and waved.

Sudden tears misted her eyes, and her heart skipped a beat. The yearning that had surfaced earlier returned, making her ache for a future that could never be.

ELEVEN

"You're very quiet, what are you thinking?" Blake asked as he steered the car back onto the highway.

His question left Christine scrambling for an answer. She couldn't very well admit she'd been having romantic thoughts about him and that the Amish women had roused her maternal instincts. "I'm sorry to leave," she responded as she watched the Amish village recede in the side mirror. "I have this gut feeling that our answer is somehow connected to this community."

Blake nodded. "I felt it, too. But it was like we were on a fishing expedition and didn't have the right lure."

"Huh?" Christine laughed. "Never mind. I think I get your point. We don't have enough information to know what we need to ask."

"Something like that."

She smiled at him. "I think our brains are just too tired. It's been a long day."

He yawned. "Indeed. That phone call was a long time ago."

"Uh-oh."

"What now?"

Christine had taken out her phone and was staring at

it. "I turned my phone off when we got to the village."
She grimaced. "I've missed fifteen phone calls from
Melinda. There are ten text messages, too."

"Did something happen?"

Christine scrolled through the texts and groaned.
"She's reminding me that I am due at the hairdresser
in an hour."

"For what?"

"For a gala I completely forgot about."

"That's easy. Tell her you're not going for safety reasons."

Christine knew Blake was concerned about her, but
this would be okay. "I have to go. Henry is one of the
hosts. You don't need to worry. It's a gala honoring top
members of Austin law enforcement. Security will be
airtight."

"Still. It's taking an unnecessary risk."

"You want to argue that with Melinda?" Christine
teased.

"Sure. Call and put her on speakerphone."

Christine tried to hide her amused expression as she
hit Call. This promised to be entertaining.

Melinda answered on the first ring, and Christine
had to hold the phone away from her ear to avoid the
blistering reprimand. When Melinda paused to catch
her breath, Christine had her chance.

"I've got Blake here on speaker to tell you why he
doesn't think it's a good idea for me to come to the gala.
He doesn't think it's safe."

"Ranger Larsen." Melinda's voice dripped honey.
"I've been so worried that I couldn't reach Christine.
She's a daughter to me, you know."

"Yes, ma'am. And that's why I'm sure you want her as safe as can be."

"Well, yes, of course. But it's very important she be at the gala tonight. She'll want to put on a brave face and show she is standing strong despite the attacks."

"With all due respect, ma'am, why should she need to prove that? Anyone who knows her is well aware of her strength. I knew her by reputation long before I met her. I guarantee no one suspects she is anything but magnificently strong."

"Well, yes, of course, but—"

"So she certainly shouldn't be risking her life because of that."

Blake glanced over at Christine and winked. It was all she could do not to laugh out loud.

"Blake, sugar, surely there couldn't be any risk to her life in a room full of the absolute finest law enforcement officials in the whole state of Texas."

Blake bit back a laugh as he mouthed to Christine, *She's good.*

"I'll tell you what, ma'am. I'll check with my superior. He should be far better versed in the security arrangements than either of us. If he thinks it's safe, and Christine wants to go, I'll escort her."

Christine buried her face in her hands. She could practically see Melinda glowing through the phone.

"You do that, Ranger Larsen. Christine, I'll expect to see you at the house as soon as you get the okay. We have to get you ready for your date."

The phone disconnected, but Christine didn't lift her head. "You had to say that?" she muttered through her palms.

Blake laughed. "Don't worry. I've dealt with my fair

share of society ladies over the years. Melinda doesn't faze me."

Well, she humiliated me, Christine wanted to retort.

Blake's call to his boss saved her from needing to reply. Christine could hear only Blake's side of the discussion, but she realized his superior must have suggested a reason for them to attend.

"Yes, I agree. That's a valid point." Silence. "Yes, I will be with her." Silence. "Yes, sir. See you there."

The call ended and Blake glanced over. "Time to get the party duds on."

"What was his valid point?"

"There were two actually. Since we suspect corruption, he thought we should keep our eyes out for anyone who might show an interest in you. He did promise that security would be at the highest level of alert."

"Okay. And the second point?"

"He'll be in attendance and he would like a chance to meet with you."

"Oh."

Christine wasn't sure how to react to that. Was he testing her to see if she was trustworthy?

"He also wants a full report on our visit to the Amish community."

"How does he know about that?"

"I called in an update while you were in the quilting shop."

Christine massaged her temples, hoping to alleviate a growing headache. "Then I guess we're going to a ball."

As they drove into Henry's neighborhood, they found security posted at both entrances to the block. Anyone entering had to show identification and names were cross-checked against a residential list.

"How long will they be able to keep this up?" Christine shook her head. "I hope it doesn't mean they're considering Henry the prime target."

Blake reached over and squeezed her hand. "No worries. You've got the Rangers on your side."

Melinda met them at the door of the newly repaired home. "The gala starts in four hours. Look at you. Where have you been?"

Christine sighed. How could she possibly answer? *First I escaped an explosion aimed at killing me. Then I went to an Amish town to investigate the murder you think I imagined.* "Good to see you, too, Mel."

Melinda continued on without interruption. "Never mind. I wish I could schedule a spa treatment, but no time." She waved her arms and released an exaggerated sigh.

Christine didn't have to look to know she was a mess. It had been a long day, and Melinda's enthusiasm overwhelmed her. "I really don't want to go to this, Mel."

"Sweetie, you have to. This is important to your career. Everyone who is anyone in Austin law enforcement will be there."

Which was exactly why, despite all her earlier protestations to the contrary, Christine suddenly didn't have the energy to attend. By now everyone knew she was on leave. Did they also know why—that she'd witnessed a murder with no body? Would everyone be staring and pointing behind their champagne glasses?

Oh, stop it. She was all out of patience with herself. It didn't really matter what anyone thought. She would put on a pretty dress and show what she was made of. But that required the energy she didn't currently have. "I need a nap."

Melinda glanced at the clock. "Fine, a quick nap, then a long bath. I'll find something for you to wear."

Christine knew she was beyond tired when she found herself agreeing to Melinda's suggestion, but an hour later, when Melinda woke her to get dressed for the ball, she regretted the impulse.

"I can't wear that."

"Of course you can."

"It sparkles." The dress was midnight blue woven with silver.

"It does. You're going to knock that Ranger's socks off."

Christine rolled her eyes. "Where is Blake?"

"Blake went home to change. Stop with the eye-rolling, you'll get wrinkles."

Christine just laughed. Melinda was doing her best to fill a mother's role, but for the life of her, Christine couldn't imagine her justice-driven mother taking time to worry about wrinkles. She had, however, taken great care with her appearance. Christine remembered sitting on her mother's bed as she dressed in one of her power suits. *It will be better for your generation, love, but I have to prove I am worthy to play with the big boys.*

Thinking of the control Henry was exerting over her career, Christine sighed. "It hasn't changed all that much."

"What's that, sweetie?"

"Nothing, Mel. Just talking to myself. You win. I'll wear the dress."

Forty-five minutes of Melinda-induced torture later, seeing the stunned look on Blake's face as she descended the stairs made Christine decide she owed Mel an apology. Although she was used to her col-

leagues admiring her brain and expertise in the courtroom, she'd never seen this look on anyone's face before.
There was no denying it felt good.

"You clean up well," Blake whispered as he took
her arm.

Joy bubbled in Christine's heart. "Not so bad yourself, Ranger. But no cowboy hat with the tux?"

"Figured they'd make me check it at the door."

Christine laughed as they stepped out the front door
and then turned to face him on the stoop, her expression serious. "I seem to be saying this a lot, but thank
you for doing this for me."

Blake cast her another appreciative glance as they
strolled down the path. "The pleasure is all mine."

"It might not be all pleasure. I'm concerned—"

He opened the car door for her, and once she was
settled, he leaned in. "No concerns. Not tonight."

Looking up at his kind face, Christine found herself
agreeing. The past few days had been hard on him, too,
and he was doing it all for her, a relative stranger.

Christine tried to remember his suggestion as she
stepped into the ballroom. Colored lights sparkled from
dazzling chandeliers, casting deep blue shadows across
the dance floor. At least her dress matched the setting.
Had Melinda planned that? She wouldn't put it past her.

"Far cry from our Amish meal this morning," she
murmured.

Blake gazed out over the room, then looked back to
her. "I preferred eating alone with you."

"It's not too late to cut out," she teased.

"Oh, no, you don't. It's not every day I get to impress
my fellow Rangers by having the most beautiful woman
in the room on my arm."

Christine felt the blush rising in her face as she rolled multiple replies around in her head. Nothing felt right. She shrugged. "I don't know what to say to that."

"I mean it, you know." He ducked his head for a moment, and she had a feeling he wished he had his cowboy hat to hide behind. "These past few days with you have been hectic, but in a strange way I've enjoyed them. Strike that. What I've enjoyed is getting to know you—the real you."

"Thank you."

"You're a pretty amazing woman. I hope all these bigwigs here know it and know how valuable you are."

Christine made a face. "Tell that to Henry."

"I will. When the time is right. For now, let's remember why we're here."

"To pretend we're having fun while we investigate," she muttered. Realizing she sounded cranky, she added an explanation. "I know this is important, but I've never been comfortable at these kinds of events." She shrugged. "I just want to do my job, you know. Schmoozing with people just to get ahead isn't my style."

"I understand. But tonight we have work to do. So let's get out there and talk to people." He took her hand and gently squeezed. "I'll be right beside you."

He was good as his word for most of the night, walking with her from one group to another, introducing her to friends, making small talk. She grew more at ease as people accepted her. Maybe Henry was wrong. Maybe everyone wasn't judging her and finding her lacking.

Even so, the pressure to appear unquestionably sane and stable was exhausting, so while Blake was deep in conversation with a group of Rangers, she excused herself. She needed a few minutes away from the crowds to shore up her defenses and ease the headache that had started to pound in her temples.

The ladies' room was blessedly empty, so Christine took time to run cool water on her wrists and touch up her makeup. She was unused to fussing about her appearance, but knowing Blake was waiting made her take just a bit more care than usual. *The most beautiful woman in the room.* Ha. But she couldn't deny it felt good to have him say so. She smoothed the straps of the gorgeous blue dress and gave a little twirl.

With her heart feeling lighter, Christine left the marble-and-gold bathroom and stepped out onto the balcony overlooking the ballroom. A sea of elegance swam before her, formally garbed men and women dazzled beneath sparkling crystal chandeliers. Music, food and beverages flowed smoothly. Some couples danced, more clustered in small circles. These were the people Henry was concerned about. These were the power brokers, the people who could make or break her career. Was there a murderer among them?

She understood why Henry was so intent on protecting her reputation, but as she stood there surveying the crowd, she realized she had a choice to make. A moral one. She was risking everything to pursue justice for a man she couldn't identify, whose body couldn't be found and, therefore, whose death couldn't be proven. Was that worth risking a career she'd spent years building?

Deep in her heart, Christine knew there was only one answer, even if it meant an end to all she had worked for.

This world, all this glittering perfection, was tainted by greed and corruption and something sinister that was making people deny what she'd witnessed. She couldn't surrender to that. She couldn't become that.

An uneasy feeling settled in her chest, displacing her joy, as she compared this scene to the simplicity of the Amish community they'd visited this morning. The quiet faith and fortitude of the women she'd met impressed her. She knew their life wasn't perfect. If it had been, she wouldn't have been there pursuing a killer, searching for a victim. Everyone's life came with struggles. It was how you chose to face them that made the difference.

Was the Amish way better than what she had chosen? Each day she used her legal skills to secure justice. She worked hard to help others have a better life. And what of the sacrifices that required? She had no personal life, no family, few friends except Henry and Melinda.

She glanced again at the sparkling ballroom full of powerful and gregarious people. It was so easy to get swept up by this life, drawn into the relationships and politics of her work. After all, wasn't that how she'd been coaxed into coming here tonight? Melinda had dangled the apple of connections—the chance to see and be seen, to connect with those in power.

Was that God's will for her life? Suddenly she was filled with doubt. This path she'd been beating all these years, this desperate desire to fulfill her mother's goals—if it meant living this glittering life, throwing herself heart and soul into this superficial culture, was that really the right way? Was it God's way?

She was doing her work for God's people. But was she doing it for Him or was she using that as justification for pursuing her own goals with mindless ambition?

Down below, Blake turned, saw her and waved.

Christine waved back and shook off the questions. They were important, but this party wasn't the place for introspection. She would pray about it, she promised herself, pray for discernment.

One trip to Amish country shouldn't have her considering throwing away a lifetime of choices. She had important work to do. If mixing and mingling was required, then that was the way it was—for now.

By the time she made it down the stairs, Blake had been waylaid by a man she didn't know. He was deep in conversation, listening attentively in that way he had of making you feel like the complete center of his attention. And yet, even across the room, he sensed her presence, glanced over and smiled sheepishly.

Christine was debating joining him or waiting on the sidelines when she felt a tap on her shoulder. She turned to see a waiter hovering, an apologetic expression on his face.

"I'm sorry to bother you, miss. I was asked to deliver this important message."

Christine smiled and thanked him as she accepted the folded note. She opened it and laughed. The note was signed Blake but had Melinda's matchmaking fingerprints all over it.

Meet me in the garden, back by the waterfall. Blake.

She glanced over in time to see the waiter handing a similar note to him, signed by her, no doubt. She watched as he read it, glanced over at her and winked.

Christine pivoted on her spiky heel and headed toward the terrace doors. She might actually have to thank Melinda for this. The chance to leave the crowd behind and spend a few moments alone with Blake in a gorgeous garden made her heart resume singing.

The sweet floral scent lured her deeper along the paved path. Her mother had never had time for a garden, but Christine had vague memories of happy times with her grandmother in a room surrounded by flowers. She rarely thought about that time in her life, the time before her grandmother had passed. Life had changed drastically after that. Her father had never been a part of their lives, but she, her mother and grandmother had once been an intricately entwined family of three. She'd lost a part of herself, first with her grandmother's passing, and then her mother's murder. Though Henry and Melinda tried to fill the gap, the losses had defined her in ways she was only beginning to understand.

Christine wandered farther along the path, wondering just exactly where this waterfall was. She could hear the sound of gently rushing water, so she knew she was heading in the right direction, but the path was getting narrow, and the lights were few and far between.

Something wasn't right.

Blake wouldn't ask her to go deep into a dark garden. He'd been too careful of her feelings. And he was too worried about her safety.

But Blake hadn't been the one to send the note, she reminded herself.

She took another few steps as panic began to curl in her stomach. The heavy humid air seemed to suck life from the flowers. The delicate scent grew cloying. Her chest tightened, and she had to concentrate to breathe slowly. No. She couldn't do this, not even for a romantic rendezvous.

She spun around and began to hurry back. She'd left the ballroom before Blake, so she'd meet him on the path, tell him she didn't like the dark, humid space.

They could still have time alone in the garden, just not in the deep, dark recesses that threatened all manner of evil.

"Where are you going?"

Christine began to run.

That was not Blake's voice, and suddenly she wondered if Melinda had really been the one to send the note. Where was Blake? Hadn't he come out? Christine stumbled as terror wrapped around her heart. Blake wasn't here. He wasn't coming. What had his note said? Where had it sent him?

And where was the promised security? She hadn't seen one guard since she'd entered the garden.

That thought came too late. She never even heard the man come up behind her, never felt his presence until his arm snaked around her shoulders and the point of his knife bit into her neck.

"You should have learned your lesson. Interfering where you don't belong will get you dead fast."

Blake used the same doors he'd watched Christine pass through and turned to walk along the terrace. He didn't see any sign of her, but his note said she'd be waiting in the library. He laughed as he followed the terrace where it wrapped around the building. He didn't really want to think too hard about why he was eager to be alone with Christine. He knew why Melinda was giving them time together, but what she wanted wasn't possible. There was no future for Christine with him. He had a family history to prove just how impossible such a relationship was. Rangers didn't make good husbands. Their jobs were too demanding, too unpredictable, too dangerous. A wife wanted someone steady, reliable, someone who came home regularly. His own mother had walked out on his father for that reason. Dylan's engagement had broken up under the pressure. That future was not for him. He was here to protect Christine, not romance her.

And yet...

It was a beautiful night, a lovely party, and they needed some downtime. Surely there was no harm in enjoying her company tonight. Except if he was truthful, he'd admit he'd been enjoying her company far too much.

Blake reached the end of the terrace. There had been no door, no entrance to a library. A vague foreboding tingled in his bones. Where was Christine? He'd watched her walk through that doorway, but there was no sign of her. He walked to the edge of the terrace and looked out over the garden that was thick with trees and shrubs. Flowering plants crowded narrow paths, and the air lay heavy. Fear seized him at the realization that Christine was somewhere out there, probably looking for him on the same wild-goose chase that had brought him to this dead end. Except hers was probably leading her straight into deadly danger.

This was why he couldn't have a relationship. He'd been so busy thinking of romancing Christine that he hadn't realized they'd both walked smack into a trap—again.

Where was she?

Blake raced back along the terrace to the last staircase he remembered seeing. He stood at the top and peered into the darkness. Christine hated darkness. He'd learned that during their time at the safe house. Now she'd been lured into it with the promise of meeting him.

He took the steps in three jumps and headed down the path.

"Christine," he called in a loud whisper. He didn't want to draw attention, but his hopes of quickly finding her in the garden were dying with each step. There were so many turnoffs, so many paths she could have taken.

Lord, help me find her. Blake didn't remember when he'd last prayed. Probably not since his mother left and his prayers for her return went unanswered. But he would fall to his knees now if it would do any good.

Please, Lord. If not for me, help me find Christine for her sake. She doesn't deserve this. She trusts You. Please show me the way to where she is.

A sound, half-strangled, like someone trying to scream, came to him from a distance. He stood silent, trying to determine the direction. A hushed angry voice was all he heard, but it was clearly coming from up ahead and off to the left.

Praying all the while, Blake charged down the path, calling out now. His only hope was to distract whoever had her, scare him away.

"Christine."

"Over here, Blake."

He surged ahead and burst into the clearing just as someone shoved her aside and dove into the underbrush.

Uncertainty ripped through him. Go after the man, or check on Christine? He glanced at where she lay crumpled on the ground, blood dripping from her neck. All thought of pursuit vanished as he rushed to her side.

"Chris, talk to me, honey." He lifted her gently into his arms and helped her to the bench. She was shaking so badly that he wrapped his arms around her and held her tight. "What did he do?" he whispered as he tried to look at her neck.

She shook her head and burrowed into his arms. "It's okay," she managed. "He only nicked me." Her breath huffed. "Because of you. You saved me. Again."

Blake drew her more snuggly against him.

"I tried to be brave. I tried to pretend I was you."

His heart broke a little at her words knowing if he'd been doing his job properly, she wouldn't have had to pretend. "Can you tell me what happened?"

He felt her nod. "I got a note telling me to meet you in the garden. I knew you didn't send it, but I figured Melinda had, that she was trying to set us up."

Blake choked out a laugh. "I had the same thought."

She pulled back a little and looked up at him. He thought he could drown in those eyes, emerald pools spilling over with tears.

"And yet we both went." She braved a smile. "I survived because I trusted you. It was dark in the garden. I knew you wouldn't ask me to meet you in a place I felt unsafe."

He closed his eyes and swallowed hard, choking back the emotion that clogged his throat. He opened his eyes and pulled on his Ranger mode. "That's true. I wouldn't. Let me see your note."

She handed it over. "See, it tells me to go to the fountain. I started that way, but the fountain is in a dark, remote area of the garden near the parking lot. I got scared. Even though I knew you hadn't really been the one to send the note, I drew strength from knowing you wouldn't ask me to go there. I turned around and headed back." She ducked her head into his shoulder again. "That's the only reason I'm still here."

Blake stared at the note until he had himself composed. Finally he lifted his gaze to hers. "Mine sent me to the library. It was signed with a heart and the initial *C.*"

"I never sign anything with a heart."

The indignation in her voice drew a smile. "Good to know." He paused. "So we both went to the garden thinking Melinda was setting us up. We were both wrong."

Neither could voice the words, but they saw it in each other's eyes, a shared sense that something really bad had just been avoided.

"Let's agree on a code so that nothing like this ever happens again," Blake prompted.

"Okay. What?"

He thought about it for a few minutes, but came up clueless. "We'll have to work on that."

"Maybe it should include Melinda's name. Oh!"

"What is it?"

"My bracelet." Christine held up the dangling pieces. "I don't usually wear jewelry except this bracelet. It belonged to my mother."

"Let me take it. I know someone who can fix it good as new." As he took the broken pieces from her hand, Blake could feel her tremble. He wished he knew someone who could fix their problems as easily as the bracelet.

TWELVE

"Someone attacked you within spitting distance of half of Austin's top cops. We need to file a report, get crime scene techs out to look for evidence."

"I know," Christine answered distractedly. "But please don't tell Henry."

The look she turned on him, those eyes wide with pleading and fear made him want to set aside his law enforcement persona and just do what she asked. He shook his head.

"Blake, these are the people I work with," she pleaded. "The people who trust me to be competent, to represent their interests in court. Some of them already think I imagined a murder. If they think I'm not capable—" She rubbed her eyes and looked up at him again. "Henry has already made it clear I'm endangering my career by continuing along this path. What do you think will happen if I claim that some person I didn't see approached me in the garden and threatened me to back off a case that according to them doesn't exist?"

He took a handkerchief from his pocket and dabbed at the blood on her neck. "There's the proof you didn't imagine this."

She looked away. "It won't be enough."

"I'll notify my boss."

She started to protest, but Blake continued. "He believes you. He's the one who has me on this case. He'll know how to handle it discreetly."

She said nothing, simply nodded her head once. Blake took off his jacket and wrapped it around her shoulders. Then he took her by the hand and led her through the service entrance into the kitchen. He stopped one of the waitresses and flashed his badge. "Is there a private room I could use to help the lady clean a cut?"

The woman's eyes widened, but she took his silent cue and didn't ask any questions. "Right this way, sir. Do you need anything? A first-aid kit?"

Blake smiled his appreciation at her. "That would be great."

She led them into the manager's office. "You'll be private here. I'll be right back with supplies."

While they waited, Blake sent off a text to his boss. A few moments later, a soft knock on the door heralded the waitress with the promised first-aid kit. She gazed past Blake to where Christine sat with her back to the mirror. "Do you need the police or anyone?" she asked softly. "There's a whole room full of them here."

Blake smiled. "I've already requested help. Thanks—" He glanced at her name badge. "Thanks, Lilah. A Texas Ranger will be coming back looking for me. Please show him to the office. And, Lilah? I appreciate your discretion."

She nodded solemnly and left them alone.

Blake opened the kit and took out some bandages and alcohol wipes. Within minutes, the door opened and his boss entered. He nodded at Blake, then focused his attention on Christine. "Ms. Davis, I'm Ranger Harris. We met earlier. Are you all right? I'm sorry for what you've gone through tonight."

Christine waved away his concern. "I'm fine. Blake is making more of this injury than it warrants, but thank you for coming."

Blake cleared his throat. "Let Ranger Harris decide. Tell him what you told me."

When Christine had finished relating the events, Ranger Harris thanked her. "I sent men out as soon as Blake messaged me. The man was probably long gone by the time my Rangers got out there, but I'll have a crime scene crew check out the garden, see if we can find any clues. If you think of anything else, let Ranger Larsen know and he can relay it to me."

He turned to Blake. "I trust you will see Ms. Davis home? I'll talk to you in the morning unless we turn something up."

Once they were alone again and Blake had finished tending her wound, he suggested they head off.

"I don't want to leave yet. I need to get back out there, show him he didn't scare me off."

"Bad idea."

"I seem to be full of them. Blake, please. Just one dance? I don't want to leave yet."

Blake didn't like the idea. Christine was acting as if she'd shrugged off the earlier danger, but he could see the tremor that belied her stubborn pride. "You think he's still here?"

"If he's not, the person who hired him is. I need to do this, Blake. I gave in to you about contacting your boss. You can do this for me. Come dance with me."

It went against every bit of his better judgment, although the idea of dancing with her, holding her in his arms and reassuring himself she was okay, was extremely appealing.

"One dance and then I'm taking you home."

One dance turned into two, and then a few more. Blake knew it was a mistake, but holding Christine in his arms felt like the best thing that had happened to either of them in a very long time. He told himself he was offering her comfort and support, but he suspected he was allowing this more for his sake than hers.

Christine smiled up at him as he twirled her around. "I think it's a good thing we have a safe house to go to tonight. I don't think I could face Melinda's scrutiny. She's been watching us dance for the last ten minutes."

Blake chuckled. "Does that mean you're ready to leave?"

She sighed. "Not really, but I guess it's time. The adrenaline is wearing off, and the day is starting to catch up with me."

"Let's go. But we're not going to the safe house."

THIRTEEN

An attack so bold, in a venue swarming with law enforcement, alarmed Blake more than he wanted to admit. Rather than risk the safe house having been compromised, he took Christine to Dylan's ranch. He was more confident in the ranch security.

Once Christine was settled in his brother's guest room, Blake grabbed a mug of coffee and headed outside. With all the thoughts and emotions roiling in his head, he was restless. He needed open space, room to think about what the next step should be.

"You've had a busy day." Dylan emerged from the darkness of the porch.

Blake nodded. "Sure have."

"Want to run it by me?"

"You want the short version or the long one?"

"That bad, huh?"

Blake glanced back at his brother leaning against the porch railing, "Started with a dead body and an explosion. Ended with a knife and a dance. In the middle was a trip to Amish country."

"You've got my attention."

Blake sank onto the porch steps and proceeded

to recap the day. He was frustrated and puzzled and wanted any input his brother could give.

An hour and several coffee refills later, he was no closer to a solution, but he knew his next step. "Will you keep an eye on her, watch the security cams? I need to talk to Henry."

Blake stood and shook himself loose. "She doesn't want to tell him what happened, but I've got no choice. He's already involved. I need to figure out if it's innocent or something more."

"Maybe you should let someone else have that conversation," Dylan suggested.

Blake spun around. "No."

Dylan smirked at him. "When are you going to admit you've got it bad?"

"What? Nope" Blake started toward the car. "Don't even go there."

Dylan strolled down the steps to walk beside him. "Be honest with yourself, if not with me. You're falling in love with her, aren't you?"

"No."

Dylan made a rusty sound that was almost a laugh.

Blake didn't respond. He didn't want to have this argument with his brother. It was hard enough having it with himself. "You know there can't be anything between us."

"Why not?"

Blake gazed out over the quiet ranch. "Isn't it obvious? Do I have to spell it out for you? Mom, Vicky."

Dylan was silent for a bit. When he spoke, his voice was hoarse. "What does Vicky have to do with this?"

Blake hesitated. He didn't want to dig up his brother's pain, but he needed Dylan to see there could never be anything between him and Christine. "Vicky ended your relationship because she couldn't handle being with a Ranger any more than Mom could."

They stood side by side staring out into the moon-lit night until Dylan's soft voice broke the silence. "Do you ever wonder if maybe we don't know the whole story about Mom?"

Blake rocked back on his heels. "Where did that come from?"

Dylan stubbed his boot against the dirt. "I'm just saying. Dad wasn't the easiest guy to live with. Or love. Maybe Mom leaving had nothing to do with him being a Ranger. Maybe it had more to do with him being him."

Blake wasn't ready to give in. He shrugged. "That didn't help you and Vicky."

Dylan heaved a sigh. "You're wrong about Vicky."

The sadness in his brother's voice stole Blake's breath. A flippant remark had been sitting on the tip of his tongue, but he bit it back and waited.

Dylan stared off into the distance. "This goes no further than us."

Confused, Blake just nodded.

"We were just friends. I didn't love her."

"Could have fooled me. You were heartbroken when she left."

"I was," Dylan admitted.

"But?"

"It wasn't Vicky my heart was aching for. I let her spin that Ranger danger story so she could save face. I was the one who broke it off when she wanted some-thing more."

Blake studied his brother wondering how he could

have grown up with him, known him all his life, and still missed something so monumental.

Dylan ground the heel of his boot into the dirt. "Don't go blaming yourself for not knowing. I made sure no one did. I'm only telling you now so you don't make the same mistake. Don't let the woman you love get away."

"Vicky's still in town. Maybe—"

"I told you. I'm not talking about Vicky."

Blake had never heard this tone in Dylan's voice. He suddenly felt like a wretch of a brother. "Then who?" he asked gently.

"Doesn't matter. I'm not sure you'd remember her. I just don't want you to make the same mistake I did. Trust me, you don't want to live with the regrets."

"The life I live, it's not conducive to marriage," Blake protested weakly. "A wife wants a husband who comes home at night."

"A woman wants a man who loves her. Who better to build a life with than someone who gets you? Christine's not like Mom. She's not a quitter, Blake. Just look at everything she's done to find this victim. How she stood up to everyone doubting her. She is one pretty special woman." He ducked his head. "Don't lose her because you're afraid."

With those parting words, Dylan started back toward the house, leaving Blake alone with his thoughts.

Who better to understand his life than someone whose job was equally demanding? She's not a quitter. The words resonated. Still, deep inside, the wounded little boy whose mother had abandoned him couldn't help wondering. Could Christine possibly care enough about him not to leave? Was he worthy of that kind of love?

Even if she did care about him, he couldn't do anything until this case was settled and she was safe. Tonight was proof of that. He couldn't live with the guilt if she died because he let himself be distracted by his feelings for her.

Dawn found Christine unable to sleep. Restless, anxious about what the day would bring, she rose, showered and dressed in jeans and a T-shirt. One thing she remembered from summers on Melinda's ranch was that people would be up and about. Life on a ranch meant working from sunup till sundown, and maybe then some. She should go help and burn off some of this excess energy.

The house seemed quiet when she went downstairs, so she grabbed a mug of coffee from the kitchen and wandered to the window.

She stared out over the vastness of the Texas countryside and tried to breathe it in. What would it be like to have a normal life in a place like this, a chance to raise a family with a man you loved?

That brought her up short. Whoa. She'd just jumped fifteen exits on the highway of life, going in the wrong direction.

Who was she kidding? Her life didn't allow for this kind of dream. She was the Ice Dragon, the defender of the weak, and a voice for the victim. She had no life outside her work.

And yet, remembering what it felt like being in Blake's arms as they danced last night, she recalled the feelings she'd had in the quilt shop in New Grange, how she wanted something more—with him. She closed her eyes, thinking back, feeling the strength in his arms, the absolute safety she felt within his embrace despite the attempts on her life. *With him.* Two words, but they summed up so much that had changed in her life.

Is it possible this is what You were bringing me to, Lord?

She was so confused. Was she too focused on her plan and not allowing for God's plan? Or was her brain trying to put God's imprimatur on her lonely heart? How was she supposed to tell the difference?

Dylan came up beside her as she sipped coffee and daydreamed. "You look like you belong here."

Christine turned to smile at him. "I wanted to go out and help, but I figured I'd get in trouble for taking a risk."

"Help?"

"I used to spend summers down on Melinda's family ranch. Tending the horses was my chore, and I thought it was bliss."

"If that's how you feel, we can put you right to work."

Christine laughed, and there was an easy silence between them for a few minutes before she voiced what she sensed in her gut. "He left without me, didn't he?"

"Yep."

She'd known it, felt Blake's absence as soon as she walked through the house. "Said it was for my own good, didn't he?"

Dylan chuckled. "Something like that."

Christine was silent for another moment. "I suppose he took my car, too."

At Dylan's nod, she rolled her eyes. "Any chance you have a spare truck?"

This time Dylan broke into a full-out bellow of

laughter. "My brother has no clue what he's gotten himself into, has he?"

She could have asked what he meant, but she could see from the twinkle in his eye that he wasn't talking about the murder investigation. "He's not interested in me that way." She dipped her head.

"Are you?"

Christine kept her face hidden. She couldn't bring herself to meet his gaze. "Doesn't matter."

"Course it does."

She looked up in surprise at that. Dylan stood, hands in his back pockets, kicking at the floor with his boot. "Give him some time, Chris. This is all new to him."

She choked. "I find that hard to believe."

Dylan shrugged and looked her in the eye. "Believe it or not, it's the truth. He's kept mostly to himself all these years."

Christine was stunned. "Why?"

"That's for him to tell you."

They stood in silence a bit longer before Christine spoke. "It's so beautiful here, so peaceful. Thanks for letting me stay last night." She heaved a sigh. "I was pretty rattled. I think Blake knew I needed a place like this to relax."

"He's got his own ranch in the hill country."

Christine's head swung around. "He does? Why didn't he take me there?"

Dylan shrugged again. "Security. Mine is better."

Christine laughed. "That sounds like sibling rivalry."

"Nah, just the truth. He doesn't spend much time there anyway."

"Why?"

"You're just full of questions aren't you?"

"Hazard of my job." Christine grinned. She gazed dreamily out the window. "I always wanted to live on a ranch. I know it's a lot of hard work, but I loved the summers I spent working. I can't tell you how many times I almost quit law school to run back to the ranch. I guess I'd idealized it as paradise on earth."

"A grass-is-greener kind of thing."

"You never answered. Why doesn't Blake spend time on his ranch?"

"Good with the follow-ups, too. Blake said you excel at your job."

"Nice diversion, but I always get my answer." She was pretty sure she saw a smile crack his face then. "So?"

"The simple answer is he's too busy being a Ranger."

"And the not-so-simple answer?"

Dylan turned and stared. She knew he was sizing her up, and instinctively she knew it mattered. She met his gaze and held it.

"Too much time alone, I think. Too much time to think. He needs to be busy."

Something shifted deep within Christine. She'd spent these past few days being grateful to Blake for his help, but she'd ignored her instincts, the sense that there was something deeper going on. "Does he have so much weighing on him?"

Dylan kicked at the floor again before looking back at her. "Those are also his stories to tell."

"He won't."

Dylan met her gaze again, and this time his eyes held a brother's love. "If you really want to know, if you care, I think you may be just the woman who can get through to him."

Before she could even think how to answer, Dylan reached into his pocket and pulled out a set of keys. "Want to go for a drive?"

Christine stared as he dangled the car keys just out of reach.

"Where did he go?"

"To see your boss."

All thought of romance fled her mind at those words. She could hear Dylan chuckling as she stormed toward the car.

"Yeah, he's finally met his match," he teased as he hopped into the driver's seat.

FOURTEEN

Melinda opened the kitchen door, jumped back and screamed.

"Oh, Blake. Be still my heart. You scared more years off me than that the scorpion I found in my slipper. What are you doing out here?" She covered her chest with a palm and made a show of slowing her breathing. "Okay, obviously you're waiting out here for a reason. Is it Christine? Is she hurt? What happened?"

"She's fine. I need to talk to Henry."

"He's in the shower. Come on in, and I'll get you some coffee. You're sure she's okay? How long have you been out there?"

"Since three a.m."

Melinda stopped midpour. "That's crazy. Why didn't you call?"

"I needed time to control my temper."

"Oh. That doesn't sound good."

She handed him the coffee, but he set it aside and paced across the room.

"What doesn't sound good? Ranger Larsen, I thought I heard your voice. What are you doing here? Where's Christine?"

Blake glared at Henry. "We need to talk."

Melinda handed her husband a cup of coffee, and he sat at the table, gesturing for Blake to do the same.

Instead, Blake stopped across from him, rested both hands on the table and leaned in. "I know you think Christine imagined a murder, but with two more attempts on her life yesterday, I want to know when you're going to believe her and turn the investigation in the right direction. Or I'm going to start asking serious questions about why you won't."

To his credit, Henry went pale. His hands shook slightly as he lifted his coffee and took a sip.

It was Melinda who spoke. "Where is she now? I asked if she was hurt and you said no."

"I said she was fine, and she is, by the grace of God. Not thanks to anyone believing her." He looked pointedly at Henry. "She's out at my brother's ranch under strict surveillance. But you know as well as I do that she won't stay there. After the explosion, I wanted—"

"Hold on, what does the explosion have to do with her? She was here getting ready for the gala yesterday, but she didn't say anything about trouble."

Blake just stared at him for a long moment. "After all the doubts you've cast on her emotional state, you're surprised she didn't mention anything?"

Henry started to stutter a reply but had the grace to stop and listen as Blake continued. "We were in the warehouse when it exploded. She was the intended victim, and before you ask how I know, I do. It's my job to investigate things like that."

Henry swallowed hard. "What happened last night? She was at the gala."

"Someone grabbed her in the garden."

Blake ignored Melinda's gasp and looked straight at Henry. "When I interrupted them, he had a knife at her neck."

"And you didn't come get me then? Did you call the authorities?"

"Do not even try to put this on me." Blake ground out the words. He'd heaped enough blame on himself in the hours he'd been waiting to talk to Henry. He didn't need the man adding to it. "Christine wouldn't let me call you. She was afraid to make a scene, afraid of losing her career."

His tone left the implied question of where she could have gotten that idea hanging. "For the record, I called the Rangers to the scene at the gala, and I took her to my brother's ranch for safety."

"You should have brought her back here."

"Give me one good reason why I should trust any part of her protection to you."

Melinda broke through the palpable tension in the air. "Blake, Henry, just stop. This is dreadful. Poor Christine. We have to do something, Henry. We've let this go on too long."

The men stared at each other in tense silence.

Blake flipped a chair around and sat facing Henry. "You've got one of Austin's finest prosecutors telling you she witnessed a murder. Instead of believing her, you put her on leave and tried to convince her she imagined it. That doesn't make me doubt her, Henry. It makes me wonder whether you're involved. Who are you really protecting here?"

Henry buried his face in his hands. "I've only ever tried to protect Christine."

"You've got a funny way of showing it. Since you

and the police insist on investigating her past cases rather than accepting she witnessed a murder, she's determined to find out for herself who murdered the man and who is behind the attacks on her."

Melinda poured more coffee, scrambled eggs and drained the bacon while the men glared at each other. She loaded two plates with bacon and eggs and set them on the table. "I told you this wouldn't work, Henry. She's her mother's daughter."

Before Blake or Henry could respond, they heard a truck pull into the driveway.

Christine burst through the door minutes later, skidding to a stop partway into the room. She surveyed breakfast on the table and the two men obviously in the midst of conversation.

"Isn't this lovely. Enjoying breakfast while you decide how to handle me?"

Blake rose and walked toward her. "Christine. Calm down. What are you doing? It's not safe for you to leave the ranch. You know—"

"You! Don't you even talk to me, and don't you dare tell me to calm down. What were you thinking taking off like that and leaving me out there? You don't get to tell me what to do." She stopped and drew a breath. "Dylan drove me. I was perfectly safe. He's keeping watch outside."

Blake bit back the retort that hovered on his lips and settled for a diplomatic one. "You needed sleep. I wanted to fill Henry in and see how we can change his investigation."

"You didn't think I should be included in that conversation?"

The look of betrayal in her eyes undid him. He'd

been so busy trying to protect her that he'd ignored her need to help herself. "I'm sorry."

"Christine." Henry stepped up between them. "Don't blame him. It's my fault. I was wrong to deny you saw something. I thought it would keep you safe, that I could keep you safe. I was wrong about that, too. I can't."

His shoulders drooped as he pleaded. "You need to leave town, go visit friends. Your law school roommate, where does she live now?"

"Colorado."

"Go visit her."

"You're wasting your time, Henry. I'm not leaving."

"Christine, listen."

"No, you listen, Henry." She paused, drew in a deep breath and gentled her voice. "I love you for what you did for me. I love you and Melinda for taking me in, for giving me a family. But I can't forget what I saw. I can't let a family be in the dark about their missing son. I can't ignore what I know."

Henry sank down on the chair, face in his hands. "Let the Rangers handle it. They don't need you."

"I need them, and I need to do this, Henry. Don't you see?"

Christine stood before him, hands on hips, and pleaded for understanding. "My mother gave birth to me, but you and Melinda, you gave me a home, and you gave me wings to fly. I can't have those wings clipped now, Henry. I need to do this. Can't you understand that?"

He was silent a long minute. "I do, Christine, but it's what you don't know that will get you killed."

He stood and paced across the room. "I felt the same

way after your mother died. But then they threatened you and my family." He shrugged. "I had no choice. A part of me died that day. So I can't give my blessing, and I can't agree with what you're doing, but I do understand."

She'd heard that story before, vague rumblings about threats, but she'd never paid it much mind. Now it dawned on her that Henry had paid a far higher price than she'd ever known. She held out her hands and took both of his. "I'm so sorry you had to make that choice. But I have nothing to lose."

She could see him thinking, debating something with himself. She squeezed his hands. He looked up, and she could see the anguish in his eyes as he began to speak.

"You're wrong. You have your life to lose. There is more to this." He released a long, heavy sigh. "There were rumors, Christine, about the man behind the gang that killed your mother, that it was Ned Rivera."

"The man who owns the warehouse?"

Henry shook his head. "His father. The rumors claimed he was involved with the cartels."

He cleared his throat. "He was also our neighbor. Melinda's family ranch borders theirs." He shook his head solemnly. "I couldn't believe it was possible. Nothing was ever proven. Time went by. He died a natural death. I forced myself to forget, to concentrate on raising you."

The room was silent, Christine, Blake and even Melinda hanging on his every word. "When I saw who owned the building where you witnessed the murder, it all came racing back. I panicked. I pulled you off duty so fast because it was the only way I knew to protect you."

Anger simmered in Christine's chest, warring with

grief, love and gratitude. "I don't need to be protected. I need the truth."

"You won't find it. You won't find proof. They know how to keep their hands clean, who to pay, how to evade detection."

Christine gritted her teeth and struggled to remember she owed Henry her life. He had acted in a way he thought best. Well, now she had to do what she thought best. If this man's family truly had been behind her mother's murder, then she would stop at nothing to bring him down.

"I love you, Henry. And I appreciate all you've done for me. But I have to do this for myself."

"Blake, how hard would it be for you to get Ranger backup?"

Startled, Christine swung to look at Melinda, who was leaning forward over the kitchen counter, her face set in an expression Christine had never seen before.

"Not hard."

"You can use my ranch—"

"Melinda, no!" Henry barked.

Melinda straightened. Her face was grim, her voice serious. "Henry, I don't like this any more than you do, but it's gone on long enough. If there had been any prayer of Christine giving in, you just squelched it. Did you really think telling her there was a connection to her mother's death would make her give up?"

Her tone implied she would have more to say about that privately, but Christine settled for being grateful she had one less person to fight. "Thank you, Mel."

Melinda crossed the room and wrapped her arms around Christine. After a quick, fierce hug, she stepped back and took Christine's face in her hands. "Make no mistake, I don't like this. But like they say, the apple doesn't fall far from the tree. Your mother knew she was in danger, but she wouldn't give up. I know you won't, either, so I'm begging you to be smart. Let the people whose job it is take the lead now. You're too smart to be dumb about this."

Christine studied the woman who had been her surrogate mother all these years. Most people took Melinda to be a flighty socialite, and she played to the stereotype, but Christine knew and loved the woman beneath the facade. Melinda understood her. She had been the silent force behind getting Henry to agree every time he'd tried to swaddle Christine in protective layers. It was Melinda who'd helped her with her law school application, and Melinda who'd convinced Henry to let her follow in her mother's footsteps. Christine owed her too much to take this request lightly.

Tears glistened in her eyes as she hugged Melinda. "I will. Thank you for everything you have ever done for me," she whispered.

Melinda stepped back, shook herself and donned her best simpering smile. "Now you, Mr. Handsome Ranger, I'm putting her life in your hands. Don't let me down."

Blake's expression held steady, despite the shadow that settled in his eyes. His voice was low and firm as he replied, but it held a tone that troubled Christine.

"I will keep her safe, ma'am."

FIFTEEN

As Melinda said, if there had ever been a prayer of persuading Christine to stop, Blake realized it was gone now that she knew about the possible connection to her mother. Still, he had to try. He glanced over at her. She'd been silent for much of the drive down, and he worried what plan she might be concocting.

"Once we're at the ranch, what are the chances of you staying holed up and letting the Rangers take care of this?"

Her laugh made his heart sink. "Christine—"

"Blake, I'm not going to do anything stupid, but you have to admit that everything we know about this case is because we dug it out, not because law enforcement did anything to help."

"But now that we know—"

"We don't know enough. Sure, it looks really obvious the Riveras are involved, knowing what Henry told us. But we still don't even know who died. We need to go back to the Amish and find out the pieces. We're still a long way from understanding what happened, why that man was killed. And they're far more likely to talk to me than someone with a badge."

She fell silent, and Blake glanced over. "What's wrong?"

"I was just thinking of the victim. I saw him get murdered, but I still don't know his name. I don't know if he's Samuel. But whether he is or not, he has family that doesn't know he's no longer alive. It just seems so incredibly sad."

Resignation washed over Blake. "You need to find the answers for them every bit as much as you want to know who is after you, don't you?" He didn't understand how it was possible to know her so well after such a short time, but he was sure of this.

"I do." She turned to face him. "Justice is a noble ideal, but if it's not real, if it doesn't positively affect people's lives on a small level, what's the point? That man has people waiting for him, wondering why he hasn't come home. I'm the one person who knows the answer."

"Which is why you are also the one with the target on your back."

She shivered. "You're not a big fan of sugarcoating, are you?"

"Not in matters of life and death."

She turned to stare out the window. Sunlight glinted off her hair and shadowed the lines of her face, and he could see the tension in her jaw. Part of him wanted to comfort her, promise to do whatever was necessary to help heal the hurt in her heart. But he'd made that mistake once before with fatal results.

Memories threatened to drag him down a dark alley, but he yanked himself back. He needed to focus on protecting Christine. That meant pushing guilt to the recesses of his mind along with this unacceptable attraction. His job was to keep her safe, and that needed to be his sole focus.

"Earth to Blake."

Christine's words broke through his thoughts.

"I'm starving." She laughed softly. "I was so busy being self-righteous that I didn't eat any of the breakfast Melinda prepared. Any chance we can stop somewhere?"

If she kept smiling and charming him, he'd have to work that much harder to keep her at a distance. The dilemma tugged at him. He couldn't be so distant that he drove her off on her own—like Sofia.

"We're pretty close to New Grange. You don't want to wait and eat at the Bylers' restaurant?"

"No, I think we need to make it a business visit this time." She checked the map on her phone. "Let's stop in the non-Amish part of town first. There's a diner. We could get something to eat and see if anyone knows anything."

He started to object, but she interrupted. "I'm sorry, Blake. I'm so frustrated. Mrs. Byler has clues. She probably knows who the man was who I saw get murdered. We need to present this as a case we're investigating."

"I understand your impatience, but the Amish are known for wanting to handle things on their own and not involve law enforcement."

Christine let out a sound that was something like a growl. "Well, that's convenient for the bad guys since they don't want law enforcement involved, either."

"Plug the change of address into the GPS. We'll go to the diner."

A short drive put them in the heart of a typical small Texas town. They exited the car, and Christine started toward the diner while he surveyed the street. Nothing here indicated any connection to the nearby Amish community, but Blake had to wonder if anyone had information. Wouldn't it be nice if someone stopped them and said, *Hey, I know exactly what you're investigating, and I know the answers?*

Christine stopped short ahead of him. "Blake." Her voice sounded like someone was strangling her. "Blake, come look at this." She was pointing to a paper stapled to the utility pole. "It's him. That's the man I saw get shot."

Blake studied the missing persons poster as Christine whispered, "It's really him."

"You're sure?"

She swallowed hard. "I am. His eyes are blue like the man I saw." She stared at the image. "He really doesn't look Amish in this photo."

"If he *was* Amish, there probably wouldn't be a photo," Blake noted.

"Good point. So probably not Samuel." Relief washed over her face. She sighed. "But he had the paper with the store's name and address." She pulled the poster off the pole. "Let's take this photo back and ask Mrs. Byler. Surely she'll at least tell us if she knows who he is."

Blake took the poster from her. "There's a number to call. We could find out that way."

"It would make sense, but could we wait and talk to her first?" She hunched her shoulders and scrubbed her face with her hands. "I don't know why, Blake, but I just have this feeling that's how we should do it."

Blake wasn't happy with the idea, but he didn't want to argue with her. "Why don't you go order the food to take out? I have some calls to make."

Blake paced outside the diner pretending to talk on his phone. He kept a wary eye on everyone who passed by, but he focused on one young man who was lingering outside a newsstand. He'd noticed the man watching as Christine tore the paper from the pole and he'd stayed still watching as she entered the diner. On a hunch, Blake dialed the number on the poster. The young man took out his phone and answered.

"Hello?"

Blake slowly walked toward him as he spoke. "I'm calling about the photo on the poster. Do you know who he is?"

He looked up and straight at Blake, then turned on his heel, ran down the street and ducked into an alley. Blake gave chase, but when he reached the end of the alley there was no one in sight. Frustrated, he returned to the diner. If the Amish couldn't shed light on the photo, he would track down that number.

Christine exited moments later with their food, and they headed back to New Grange, where the welcome was decidedly less warm than on their first visit.

Mrs. Byler was polite but wary as Christine sat across from her in a back room off the restaurant's kitchen.

Christine folded her hands in her lap to keep from fidgeting as she spoke. Blake stood behind her. "Thank you for seeing us, ma'am."

Mrs. Byler nodded. "You said it was important."

Christine gathered herself. "Mrs. Byler, I don't want to bring you trouble. I didn't want trouble myself, but I saw a man murdered, and I can't find it in my heart to ignore that."

The woman eyed her quizzically. "You think it has something to do with us?"

"I don't know that it does, except for two things. The man who was killed was carrying a scrap of paper with the name of your store on it." Before the woman could respond, she continued. "We also found this poster on a tree in town. Do you know this man?"

Christine heard a gasp behind her and turned to see Rebekah staring at the photo with her hand over her mouth. "Johnny."

"Do you know him?"

Mrs. Byler answered. "That young man is an *Englischer*, a friend of my son, Samuel. His name is John Carter. They met during Samuel's *rumspringa* times. John comes by sometimes to help Samuel with his woodworking."

Chills raced down Christine's spine, and goose bumps broke out along both arms. "I know you said he was not here the other day, but it would be very helpful if we could talk to Samuel."

"I'm sorry. That's not possible."

Christine started to object, but Mrs. Byler interrupted her.

"Ms. Davis. My son disappeared a week ago. We have no idea where he is."

That news set Christine back in her chair. She looked up at Blake who stepped forward.

"Mrs. Byler, have you heard from him at all?" When the woman slowly and sadly shook her head, Blake prompted, "Have you called the sheriff?"

She shook her head again. "No. No to all those questions."

Christine's shock must have shown on her face, because the Amish woman addressed what she was thinking.

"Ms. Davis, we trust in the goodness of the Lord. He knows where Samuel is."

Christine couldn't even imagine how to react. She couldn't fathom that level of faith, of trust. "But—"

"I understand it is not your way. You have gone to much trouble seeking answers, but that is not our way. We wait and pray. It does not mean a lack of concern. We trust in the Lord."

Christine was struggling to find a way to stay respectful, but she couldn't walk away without more answers. She wondered if Rebekah could add anything, but when she turned to look for her, she realized the girl had slipped from the room. "Rebekah seemed upset."

"Ms. Davis, you just told us you strongly suspect you witnessed this man being killed. He was my son's friend. Is it any surprise my daughter is upset?" The woman's voice was calm and patient, while Christine's emotions were on the opposite end of the spectrum. Rebekah's reaction, she understood. She would like to talk to the young woman, see if she knew anything more.

"There is one thing."

Christine noticed that Mrs. Byler had twisted the sewing in her lap and wondered if she was quite as calm as she had claimed.

"A man has been by several times asking for Samuel." She hesitated. "I hadn't paid it much mind because it was business, but..." Her voice cracked. "Considering John is dead, it does concern me. But what choice do we have? It is in God's hands."

"I mean no disrespect, Mrs. Byler, but could you consider that perhaps it is God's plan that I am here? I was in that building when Johnny was killed," Christine said, using the diminutive Rebekah had called him. She started to shake as she said the words. *Johnny*. He had a name.

Blake's hand rested on her shoulder, settling her. She drew in a breath for calm.

The older woman nodded gravely. "I understand. I will speak with the bishop about it. I don't know what help we may be, but I must check with him."

Blake stepped up. "Ma'am, you've probably figured this out by now, but I'm a Texas Ranger. I know you would prefer to handle this on your own, but there is an ongoing murder investigation that you are now a part of."

Christine watched the woman's eyes widen. She hated disrupting the peace of this small community, hated that they had brought the outside world in. Still, she wasn't the one who had killed Johnny. And why was Samuel missing, as well? Could he be involved somehow?

And what of Rebekah? Clearly the girl knew something she was not sharing in front of her mother.

Blake's voice broke into her thoughts. "May I go with you to see the bishop? I believe this is a matter of some urgency, and there is danger to anyone who was involved."

Blake's words, coupled with the authority of his badge seemed to shake the woman more than all of Christine's pleas. She nodded her agreement. "But just the two of us please."

When Blake objected, Christine had other ideas. "I know you want me to come, too, but let's not overwhelm the bishop with our case."

Blake looked suspicious as Christine feigned inno-
cence. "You and Mrs. Byler go. Both of us would be
overkill."

His expression warned her not to do anything foolish. "I'll be fine here, Blake. It's perfectly safe." Well,
except for one man dead and another missing. "No one
knows I'm here."

As soon as Blake and Mrs. Byler left, Christine
rushed into the shop. "Did either of you see where Rebekah ran off to?"

The girls looked at each other and shrugged.

"She was very upset, wasn't she?"

At that they nodded. *"Ja."*

"That's why I need to speak with her. Please, if you
have any idea where she might have gone…"

The younger girl laughed. "She probably went to
Samuel's workshop. She likes to pass time there, avoiding chores."

Christine smiled because the impish expression was
so universal. She knew the girl was hinting at a love
interest. Was that why Rebekah had run out so fast?
She couldn't even allow her thoughts to go there. How
horrible.

"Can you point me to the workshop?"

The older girl guided her to the door and pointed
down the road. "See that house all the way at the end?
That's his shop. It's on the edge of town so the warehouse worker can back in with his truck."

Christine spun around. "What warehouse worker?"

"The one who sells the furniture Samuel makes. He
comes down from Austin with his big truck, loads up
the furniture and heads back."

Christine hurried down the street. Despite her promise, she couldn't wait for Blake to return. This was too important. She had a hunch they were so very close to figuring out what had happened, and Rebekah may well hold the key. Besides, she reassured herself, the killers had no way of knowing she had come here.

When she reached the shop, she ran up the two steps and tried the door. Locked. She ran over to the big front window and tried to peer in, but it was completely dark.

Christine tried to put herself in Rebekah's shoes. Amish or not, receiving news of a friend's death would be shocking. She probably wanted to be alone, so she wouldn't have turned lights on. But how had she gotten in if the door was locked?

The girls said a truck pulled up to the back to pick up furniture, so there had to be a back entrance. She hurried around the side of the building and skidded to a stop. There was a truck parked there, but it wasn't a furniture delivery truck. It was a standard pickup that might be seen on any ranch. Why was it here? Any other place, a parked truck wouldn't rouse suspicions, but hidden behind an Amish store?

Christine was about to turn back to get Blake when she heard a voice.

She stepped to the doorway and peeked in. Although she couldn't see anyone, she heard the tremor in Rebekah's voice.

"I'm sorry, sir, Samuel isn't here today. If you care to leave your name, I can have him contact you when he returns."

Christine stepped into the room just as she heard a fist slam against something.

"Where is he?"

Her blood ran cold and, she quickly ducked behind an armoire. She knew that voice. That slow, angry drawl.

"I'm sorry, sir. I don't know. I've told you before, I don't work here. I just stopped by to—"

The crash of furniture drove Christine out of hiding. This man had killed Johnny. She couldn't leave Rebekah to the same fate. Uttering a prayer for help, she ran for the front of the store where the man had Rebekah up against the counter.

"Leave her alone."

He whirled around.

"You!" he growled at the same moment Christine realized she finally had a face to go with the voice. A face for the man who had been tormenting her this past week.

He charged toward her, but Christine was faster. Fueled by adrenaline, she turned on her heel and dashed for the back of the store. Mentally apologizing to Samuel, she scattered hand-carved chairs behind her as she ran. She couldn't help the flash of glee when she heard a howl after her pursuer ran into the first piece. There was something to be said for the hard wood and strong construction of Amish furniture.

She dashed into an open workroom and bolted the door. Once inside, she pulled her phone from her purse. She had to call Blake before the man broke through.

Her fingers trembled as she heard the explosion from his gun. A bullet embedded itself in the hardwood paneling. Christine prayed and searched for somewhere to hide as he emptied the gun's chamber into the door.

The storeroom provided plenty of options, and she sent prayers of thanks winging toward heaven as she wedged herself into a corner between a bureau and a bookcase.

With shaking fingers, she hit Blake's name in her contact list.

"Christine, where are you? We heard shots."

Relief poured through her. "It's him. He's here." Suddenly she was terrified. She had run to draw his attention from Rebekah, and she could only hope the Amish girl had taken the time to escape. "He had Rebekah."

"Rebekah is fine. She's here with us. Where are you?"

"I'm in the storeroom. But don't come in here. I don't know where he went."

Glass shattering behind her provided the answer. She lowered her voice to a whisper. "I think he just broke a back window. I can't see him yet, but I know he's here."

"Hang on, I'm coming."

"Blake, don't. I don't want you to get hurt. He has a gun."

She thought she heard him sigh. "So do I. This is my job, remember?"

Christine bit down on her lip. She imagined there was a lot more he'd be saying about that once she made it out of here. *If* she made it out of here.

Footsteps echoed through the room, and panic threatened to consume her. Her heart was pounding so hard she was sure he could hear it. *No.* She'd come too far in overcoming her anxiety. She could do this, fight the fear. *Help me, Lord. You are my strength.*

"Time's up, Ms. Davis. You had your warning. This little game is over."

His words had an oddly calming effect. She'd been telling Blake she could protect herself. Here was her chance to prove it. This wasn't an unseen threat anymore. The man was here, in the flesh, and he was coming for her. She had an advantage as long as she kept her wits about her. She knew where he was, but he couldn't see her. His next words proved it.

"You were in the wrong place at the wrong time. It's your misfortune, because that mistake is going to have a pretty high price." He laughed, and the pure evil of it sent chills through Christine even as it strengthened her. She was not giving in to this man. Evil would not win today.

She made sure her phone was set to silent and held herself perfectly still. He was pacing the room, peering behind furniture. She knew it was just a matter of time until he got to where she was hiding. The only question was if Blake would get here first. She needed to end it before that. She didn't want Blake risking his life for her even if it was his job.

With slow and silent moves, she picked up one of Samuel's heavy wooden planes and sent it sliding across the floor. As the man swung in that direction, Christine jumped up and shoved the heavy bookcase with all her might. It crashed against him, knocking him down enough that she could fly past him and out the door.

She took off around the building and ran down the street, ducking into the yard behind another building. She could hear Blake's shouts from the front of the building and the sound of gunfire being exchanged. Long moments passed before she heard a truck roaring to life. He was escaping! She groaned. Why hadn't she thought to write down the license plate?

"Christine?"

Blake's voice calling her name was the most beautiful sound she'd ever heard. "I'm over here," she whispered, repeating it in a voice he could hear.

She ran out to the street and straight into the arms that were waiting for her. Blake closed them tightly around her. "Are you okay? Did he hurt you?"

"Yes, no," she murmured against his chest.

He pulled back. "Let me look at you."

The look on his face was so anxious that Christine couldn't help reaching up to stroke his cheek. "It's okay. I'm fine. I told you I could protect myself."

Rather than smiling back at her as she'd hoped, he shook his head and let her go. "We'll talk about that later."

His phone rang, and he stepped away from her. "Yes, Larsen here."

She could hear him explaining what had happened, at least from his perspective. He was making arrangements with the Rangers. Suddenly she felt cold and alone.

"Ms. Davis, why don't you come with me?"

Christine looked up to see one of the Amish women she'd met in the quilt shop. "I'm Mrs. Troyer, the bishop's wife. Ranger Larsen is going to be busy a while. Come with me, and we'll get you cleaned up."

Christine glanced down. Her clothes were fine, but she was coated in a layer of sawdust. She raised a hand to her hair and could tell she had some there, too. "I must look a fright."

"You look like a brave young woman. Rebekah told us how you saved her from that man. Thank you."

Christine glanced over to where Blake paced, still talking into his phone. He turned in her direction, but his expression chilled her heart.

SIXTEEN

"Are you going to tell me what's wrong or are you going to ruin a perfectly lovely evening sulking?"

Blake had been staring at the cows grazing peacefully in Melinda's pasture. He looked up to see Christine standing in the doorway, hand on hip, ready for a fight. He met her gaze with a questioning look. "Sulking?"

She shrugged. "That's how it feels."

"Since when is it sulking to object to the person you're trying to protect going off on a wild-goose chase endangering her life?"

She came out onto the patio and stood in front of him, leaning back against the railing. "I appreciate everything you have done for me, but no one said it's your obligation to keep me safe. And for the record, I didn't go off on some wild-goose chase. I went to talk with Rebekah. How was I supposed to know he would be there?"

She was magnificent, standing there with the setting sun behind her, fierce and ready to take him on. Blake hadn't the heart to fight about this, though. How could he explain that it wasn't an obligation, it was what was in his heart? How could he tell her what he'd felt to hear the gunshots knowing she was the target? In the minutes she'd been trapped, he'd relived the guilt of Sofia's death a thousand times.

"I can't let other people fight my battles for me Blake. I have to be able to stand up for myself."

He fought to keep his voice level. "Everyone needs help, Christine."

"Knowing that and wanting it to be true are two different things. I've been alone a long time. I have only myself to rely on. I need to know that can be enough."

Blake was quiet, weighing his words before he spoke. He could hear the painful truth behind what she was saying, yet it didn't change anything. He leaned back in the chair and stared up at her. "Did it ever occur to you that knowing how to protect yourself may not be the same as actually having to do it with no help? I have full confidence in my abilities as a Ranger, but I wouldn't rush in to certain situations without backup from my team."

Christine shifted restlessly. "Point taken. You also wouldn't expect your team to eliminate you and do your job without you."

He had to give her that, though not completely. "The difference is it's not your job. It is mine."

She exhaled harshly. "This is where we always butt heads. Why can't you accept that I need to be a part of this, see it to its finish?"

"It's too dangerous."

Her eyes narrowed, and her posture stiffened. "What did she do to you, Blake?"

He kicked back and put his boots on the ground. "What are you talking about?"

Christine stepped forward until she stood in front of

him. "You've hinted about it enough. Everything about this screams some past experience. Who was she? What did she do that you can't trust me?"

Blake's gut twisted. "What did my brother say?"

"Don't try to blame Dylan. He should have told me as payback for you foisting me off on him and then disappearing. He didn't." She looked away. "He said it was your story to tell."

"It's not a story"

"It's not just a job, either. I get that." She didn't need to say anything else. He saw that she understood. In some ways, despite only knowing him a short time, Christine seemed to instinctively understand him in a way no one else ever had.

Talking about this was hard, but she was right. Every reaction he'd had on this case had been shadowed by his feelings of failure about Sofia. Since it was Christine's life on the line, she deserved to know at least the basic facts.

He stood, took a deep breath and lowered his head, tilting it away from her gaze. He didn't think he could bear to see the look in her eyes as he revealed his failure.

"The story was public, so this isn't exactly news. We were working a case that was a combination drug trafficking and domestic abuse. The man had a wife and three young children. She came to us and was working to give us evidence against him."

He heard Christine's indrawn breath. "That's hard. What made her turn on him?"

Blake backed away and paced across the patio. This was not a story he could relate standing still. "Teachers in the older girl's school reported suspected abuse. It was investigated, but the father was not home. No one

could find him. Apparently, it angered him that anyone had interfered in his family, so when he returned,
he beat her pretty badly for what he called ratting him
out to the teacher. He got drunk and beat her again,
broke her arm." He paused and swallowed the knot in
his throat.

"Sofia managed to get the kids out of the house and
to the hospital. That's where we came in. She offered
to give evidence against him for drug trafficking if we
would protect her children."

He sighed. "In hindsight, I can see what I should
have seen then. She wanted protection for her children,
but not herself."

He shook himself. "I don't know why I'm giving you
all these details. You work in the legal system. You've
probably heard of the case."

She nodded slightly. "I have, but not your perspective on it. Go on," she nudged.

Blake picked up his coffee and took a long swig. "She
told us what she knew, and we arranged a sting. She
and the children were safely in protective custody. We
set up a ring of law enforcement around the perimeter
and were just waiting for him to surrender."

"I didn't know that was your case."

Blake dared a look at her. He could see in her expression that she knew the outcome. He closed his eyes.
"I was the Ranger in charge of Sofia and the children.
I'm the one who didn't read her intentions well enough
to save her life."

"You couldn't have known."

"I should have known."

"No, Blake. You're right. I do know the case. And
I also know victims. Sofia was a victim, but she was

wily. She'd been dealing with him for years. Nothing you could have done would have changed what she was determined to do."

"She thought she could save him. That he would be grateful she tipped him off." He hung his head, and his words were muted in his chest. "It was all there, in a letter she left us. She was going to distract us so he could escape and then meet up with her later. She said she'd done what she had to do to protect her children, but that she couldn't live without the man she loved."

He repeated the last sentence, his tone a mix of self-disgust and sadness. "She walked right away from our protection and back into the arms of the man who killed her. He had no such romantic ideals about their reunion. He cursed her as a traitor and shot her dead in front of dozens of law enforcement officials." He swallowed hard. "I will never forget that moment as long as I live."

"Blake, look at me."

He wanted to say no, but that seemed cowardly. If she was disgusted by his failure, he needed to see it and own it. He took a deep breath and met her gaze.

Her expression softened before his eyes.

"You trusted her?"

He collapsed onto the patio chair. "I did. I shouldn't have. I should have understood she had a victim's mentality. I should have protected her."

Christine knelt beside him. "I know it's not possible to completely understand unless you've been there, Blake, but I don't think you could have stopped her. Even if you had stopped her that night, she would have found him another day. It sounds like she had this all planned out."

"My brain knows that."

She laid a hand on his arm and gazed up at him. The compassion in her eyes unlocked his pain. He knew his heart was in his eyes as he continued. "I don't know why I'm telling you this. I never talk about it. Even Dylan only knows part."

"I hope because you knew I'd understand." She squeezed his hand. "I can't know exactly what you're going through, but I know how hard the struggle is when your thinking brain is saying one thing, but your body, your nervous system, your whole being is in a fight-or-flight adrenaline rush. You can't trust what you feel. You can't plan for a future because you don't know if you can handle it. You can't think beyond getting through this moment."

Heavy silence fell between them.

"You're not the only one who made mistakes," she finally said softly. "I've been thinking of someone, a witness we had to put in witness protection. I didn't understand what it was like for her to have to give up everything in her life." She fell quiet again, but finally cleared her throat and continued. "At the time, we thought she was part of it. Remember that attempted kidnapping I told you about? They mistook me for her. That's when I learned how she felt. It's not like your case, but I struggle with how I treated her. Like you, I was so focused on the obvious victims that I didn't realize she was one, too."

"You believe in a forgiving God?" Blake asked softly.

"I do."

"Then forgive yourself."

She smiled weakly. "That's not so easy, is it? I'm much better at forgiving others."

Didn't he know it? He was great at doling out advice

and failed miserably in following it himself. Forgiving others was easy compared to forgiving yourself.

"Can I ask you something?" At his nod, she continued. "Have you prayed about it?"

"No." Other than the frantic prayers he'd offered in the garden, he hadn't prayed for decades.

He looked away and stared out over the ranch again. The sun was behind them, and the combination of reflecting sunlight and clouds created a majestic display of light shooting through clouds. He used to think that was the hand of God reaching down. Once, he would have praised God for such glory. Somewhere along the way, he'd stopped noticing such things, stopped giving praise.

"I don't know how I would have survived the past few years without praying," Christine murmured. "I keep thinking of the Amish family and their complete trust in God. Their son is missing, but they haven't called in the police or the Rangers. They simply pray for God's will and accept that."

She rose and walked over to the railing and stared out at the last rays of the setting sun, before turning back to face him. She rested her hands on the rail behind her back. "I pray, but I don't know how to reach that level of trust."

Blake wandered over and stood beside her. As they watched the sun set in a blaze of glory over the ranch house, he rested his arm around her shoulder, and she leaned her head into him.

"Do you think it's possible to trust like that if you weren't raised that way?"

She tilted her head up at him. "I don't know. But I

want to find out. I think it means learning to put God's will above our own."

He chuckled. "Not so easy for those of us with strong wills, is it?"

She gazed deeply into his eyes, and her lips curved in a rueful smile. "I guess we have to try harder."

When she looked up at him like that, she stole his breath. He couldn't focus on her words because it took all his willpower not to kiss her. It would be so easy to get lost in her eyes, in the emotion that welled there. Dylan was right. He was falling in love with her. Despite all the reasons it was wrong and all the warnings his brain shouted, his heart was opening to hers in a way that was completely unacceptable.

The thought rocked him, and he pulled back abruptly. He was a Texas Ranger. He would protect her, but he couldn't love her.

Christine watched Blake walk away through eyes clouded with tears. For just a moment she'd thought he was going to kiss her. She'd let herself hope, but it was a foolish hope. They were so much alike in so many ways, which was probably a huge part of the problem. It could also be part of the solution, her heart cried.

Except Blake had effectively shut her out. Christine turned to stare out over the darkening ranch. A quick movement behind one of the outbuildings caught her eye.

"Blake," she whispered.

He kept walking.

"This isn't about us. There's someone out there."

That got his attention, and her heart cracked a little more, but she didn't have time to focus on him being more worried about danger to her person than breaking her heart. A shot shattered the mug he'd set on the table.

"Down."

Blake quickly extinguished the candle and joined her on the floor. Another shot rang out. A third shot from a different direction was followed by a door slamming and the sound of a truck driving off.

When Christine started to get up, Blake held her down. "Wait. I don't trust this."

Christine didn't want to stay down beside him. She was too aware of how close they were to each other. His head was just beside hers. If he turned...

"Can you crawl through the doorway?" Blake whispered. "Find some solid furniture to get under or behind, but don't stand up."

When she had crawled into the room and crouched behind the sofa, he followed her into the room, clicked the lock on the door and stood guard beside it.

"Christine, are you okay? What happened?" Recognizing Luis's voice, she stood up and started for the hall door.

"Don't." Blake growled.

The pure force of his will sent her back behind the sofa while he flipped the lock on the door.

"It's Luis, the foreman."

"I don't care who it is. I'm trusting no one."

"I've known him all my life."

The foreman started pounding on the door. "Christine. Are you okay? What's going on in there?"

Blake came over beside her and whispered. "We don't know if he's alone. Someone could be holding a gun on him. Wait here. I'm going to go out the back and come around behind him. If it's safe as he says, I'll call to you to open the door."

Christine stared at him, her eyes wide at where his thought process was taking them. Had she brought danger to Melinda's ranch? She nodded her acquiescence. "But at least let me answer or he'll break the door down."

Blake agreed. "Give me a few minutes to get out around the patio."

Christine counted slowly to three hundred before calling out, "I'm fine, Luis. Give me a minute and I'll open the door." She waited what felt like a lifetime until finally she heard Blake's voice giving her the okay.

He and Luis entered the room together. Luis ran and gathered her into his arms. "I was so worried, *mija*, when I heard those shots. I fired back, but they took off. You are not hurt?"

"I'm fine," she reassured him.

Blake hung back as Christine explained what had happened. When she finished, Luis turned to Blake and offered his hand for a shake. "*Gracias a Dios* that Christine was not hurt. But what do we do now?"

"I called for backup earlier today. They should be here in an hour or so. In the meantime, we need to find out if anyone saw the truck or the gunman."

"I will check with my men."

Christine could tell Blake wasn't happy with the idea but had no options.

"You can go with him. I promise I'll stay here."

He looked torn. She felt defeated. "You can trust me. I've had enough excitement for one night. I'll just sit here with my computer and catch up on my caseload." She allowed emotion to show in her eyes. "Promise."

Blake nodded abruptly and walked away.

Long hours later, when the backup Rangers had settled into their posts and Blake had questioned the ranch hands to no avail, Christine tried to talk to him about their plans. She'd had those hours to think once she'd realized Henry hadn't yet restored her system access. "We must be getting too close for comfort, if they were willing to risk an attack here."

Blake turned his tired gaze on her. "I don't find that particularly reassuring."

"Don't be discouraged," she murmured. "We're finally making progress. We know who the man was whose death I witnessed. We better understand the connection to the Amish community, and we know the neighboring ranch owner is involved." She sighed. "We just need to find a way to prove it."

"There's no *we* anymore, Christine. Your part in this is done."

Christine shook her head, hoping she'd heard him wrong. His somber expression crushed that hope. "You can't mean you're cutting me out now?"

"That's exactly what I mean. You've said all along that you'd back off if someone believed you and investigated. Well, now you have all the Texas Rangers I could summon. Henry finally admitted why he put you on leave. You can have your job back. There's no reason you need to be involved any longer."

Christine couldn't believe what she was hearing. On some level, she knew he was right, but still she fumed as she paced across the floor. "You're no different than any of the other men I've had to fight for my career. Tuck the little lady home on the ranch where she can stay safe."

Blake heaved himself off the sofa and planted himself in her path. As she swung toward him, he confronted her. "You know that's not what this is about, Christine." He gentled his voice. "I respect you too much to sideline you for anything less than your safety. You've been amazing this whole time, brave, fearless even when I know the toll it has taken on you."

He opened his arms, and as much as she longed to lose herself in his embrace, she held herself stiff. He dropped his arms, and she suddenly wished she'd stepped into them while she'd had the chance.

He reached and took both her hands in his. "I need to know you're safe, Christine. I need you to promise you won't do anything foolish."

Her heart cracked at his words as she recognized the pain they were rooted in. "I won't do anything foolish, Blake. You have my word on that. But I don't want to lose you, either. You got dragged into this because of me. How am I supposed to live with myself if something happens to you?"

"I'll be fine. It's my job to do this."

There was that word again. Knowing she probably didn't want to hear his answer, she nonetheless drew herself up straight and met his gaze. "Is that all I am to you, Blake? A job?"

She saw his jaw clench, noted the struggle in his eyes, and hope sprouted. Fragile feelings she was only beginning to allow herself stirred in her heart. She reached up to brush the hair from his brow and felt the tremor pass through him.

He rested his hand around hers and pulled it gently away from his face. "I'm sorry. You have to understand. I can't let it get personal. If I have to choose, then I am a Ranger."

Christine dipped her head so he couldn't see the sheen of tears in her eyes. With as much dignity as she could muster, she walked down the hall to her room and closed the door quietly. She sank back and slid down the wall until she collapsed into herself on the floor. Only then did she let the tears begin to fall.

This was what she got for opening her heart, for losing track of her goal. She'd thought Blake was different. They were so alike, so devoted to serving others. She'd thought they understood each other. She'd thought maybe they could build a future together.

But he'd made it perfectly clear—not only was there no future, he was not even allowing her the present.

She lost track of how long she sat there in the dark, her heart shattered, her head spinning with ways to work this out.

SEVENTEEN

"Good morning."

Blake looked up from his breakfast. He could see from the expression on Christine's face that he hadn't had nearly enough coffee yet to face whatever argument she was about to present.

Christine crossed to the counter and poured her mug of coffee. He waited while she added cream and sugar, walked back to the table and sat across from him.

She was beautiful, but this morning she looked fragile, as if she'd slept no more than he had last night. He hated that his words were probably the cause, but for her safety, he couldn't give in to his feelings.

She took several small sips before she set the mug aside and lifted her face. He could almost see her shutting off all emotion as she marshaled her thoughts. When she finally spoke, her voice was soft, though firm. He had a feeling it was her courtroom closing-argument voice, and she was about to unleash the full persuasive effect on him.

"In listing all your reasons why I shouldn't be included, you neglected the one reason I have to be."

"What's that?" he asked tiredly. Didn't she understand it would make no difference? That he couldn't allow whatever it was to change things.

"My mother. These men are related to the man who had my mother murdered. You cannot possibly expect me to sit here and wait while you go after them."

Not for the first time Blake resented Henry for telling her that connection. "He said likely connected. Nothing was proven."

"And nothing ever will be as long as law enforcement runs scared from them."

"Ouch."

"I don't mean you and the Rangers," she muttered. "You've been the only ones who supported me through all of this. But don't you understand?" She turned pleading eyes on him. "This isn't just about me or the murder I saw anymore. It's also about justice for the man who killed my mother."

Blake couldn't let himself respond to the look in her eyes. He leveled his gaze. "Justice? Or revenge?"

Christine sank back in her chair, and he ached to wipe the hurt from her face. If anyone was entitled to revenge, she was.

"No." She shook her head slowly, and he realized she was actually considering his question. "No, I don't think I'm seeking revenge. I had to learn years ago to move on from my mother's murder, to forgive whoever killed her. A wise woman from church taught me that I would be letting them kill me, too, if I didn't forgive and let it go. She promised me that my mother wouldn't have wanted that for my life."

"Would she have wanted you risking your life to catch her killer?"

She crumpled. "That is just manipulative, Blake. I wouldn't have taken you for cruel."

"You don't really know me, do you?"

Her expression grew wary. She started to respond and stopped when her focus settled on a package beside her plate. "What's this?"

She picked it up and unwrapped the paper toweling, revealing her mother's bracelet. "Oh! When did you have time to get it repaired?"

He shrugged. "I couldn't sleep, so I went out to the barn, found some tools and repaired it myself." He had no intention of telling her it was his way of atoning for the tears he'd heard when he'd stood by her door last night.

She slipped the bracelet on her wrist. "Thank you." She stood and gazed at him with a strange expression on her face. "Do I really know you? Perhaps not." She shrugged. "Or perhaps I know you better than you want to admit."

She pushed her chair in. "Thank you, Blake." She held up her wrist where the bracelet dangled. "This means the world to me."

She left the room. The screen door slammed as she headed out to the paddock, and it unleashed memories buried deep in his heart. That sound, a screen door banging shut, was his last memory of his mother. She'd argued with his father yet again, but that time she stormed out, slamming the door behind her. They'd never seen her again.

Old heartache tried to rear its head, but he pushed it down. Christine wasn't walking out on him. During the long hours when he'd worked repairing her bracelet last night, he'd thought a lot about Dylan's advice, and he'd made himself a promise. If he stayed focused, kept emotion at bay and resolved this case, then—and only then—would he allow himself to see if he and Christine could have a future together.

He hoped he hadn't just put that future in jeopardy, but he didn't know any other way to convince her to stay out of the investigation. He had to keep her safe and alive. If necessary, he could live without her in his life, but he knew without a doubt he wouldn't survive if she met Sofia's fate.

"Blake?" A knock on the kitchen door drew his attention. The Rangers who had stayed over in the bunkhouse had arrived to plan their next move, one that definitely did not include the assistant US attorney.

Christine heard the door slam behind her, and it felt like her future closing off. In these few short days, she'd grown to care more for Blake than any other man she'd ever known. No matter what he said, she knew he wasn't cruel. Did he think she couldn't see through his manipulations, get that he was trying to drive her away?

She dangled the bracelet, watching the designs glimmer in the morning sunlight. "I think you would like him, Mama. He's a good man." An infuriatingly obtuse one, but a good man.

Her phone rang, and when she fished it from her pocket it read unknown caller. "Hello?"

"Ms. Davis? This is Rebekah."

The girl's voice sounded timid, unsure. "How are you calling me, Rebekah?"

"Samuel has a phone in his woodshop for business. Ms. Davis, can you come to town? There's something I need to show you. I'll be at the quilt shop."

Christine thought of her promise to Blake. "I can't. Not unless—"

"Please, Ms. Davis. I don't know who else to talk to. It's… It's about Johnny."

"Rebekah, I—"

"I have to go. Please come."

Christine heard the click as Rebekah disconnected the call. What could she do? After the way Blake had just dismissed her, he was the last person she wanted to go to; however, as much as she would love to avoid telling him about this call, she had promised not to do anything stupid. Running into town without telling him definitely fell under stupid.

Reluctantly, she started back toward the house. He wasn't in the kitchen, but voices from the den drew her, and she found him huddled with the group of men who had come to be his backup. She knocked on the door. He looked up, and impatience furrowed his brow.

"Blake, I need to talk to you."

"This isn't a good time, Christine."

"But—"

He frowned. "We're in the middle of something here."

"That's what I need to talk to you about."

Blake excused himself from the group and came over to her. He walked with her back into the kitchen. He sighed, and she felt his anguish even before he began to speak. "I told you, you're out of this now."

She gave one last try. "It's important."

He didn't even look at her. "Christine, I'm trying to understand how you feel, but if it comes down to your feelings versus your safety, you know what I must choose."

Pain lanced her heart. She didn't doubt why he was acting this way, but she was an assistant US attorney. She couldn't allow him to dismiss her. Did he not understand that working through dangerous situations actually did come with her job territory? Much as it broke her heart to acknowledge it, Blake would not always be there to protect her.

She turned and slowly walked back outside. This time she shut the door softly, hearing more finality in that click than in the resounding slam earlier. Rebekah needed her. If Blake wouldn't listen, then she'd have to figure out her own way to get there. She walked to the paddock where Luis was working with the horses and climbed up on the fence, leaning her chin on the railing as she debated what to do.

"¿Qué tienes, mija?"

She summoned a sad smile at Luis's pet name for her. "I need to go to the Amish town, and Blake's too busy to take me."

"I would take you myself, but I'm meeting with someone about the horses. I could have Roberto drive you."

A genuine smile burst across Christine's face. "Roberto is old enough to drive?" The last she remembered, the foreman's son had been a tiny boy tagging along after his father, trying to prove he could do everything his papa did.

Luis grunted. "He thinks he's old enough for a lot of things, but *sí*, he can drive the truck."

Christine jumped down. "That would be great." A little voice in her head warned that she was taking an unacceptable chance, but the voice was drowned out by the pain in her heart. With her own life in ruins, if she could help someone else, she was willing to take the risk.

By the time Roberto pulled the truck around, Christine was buzzing with impatience. She gave him a quick hug, hopped in and told him where they were going. They passed a truck coming up the long drive. Was Blake expecting someone else?

"That's the foreman from a neighboring ranch. He's here to talk to Papa about some troubles we've been having."

"Really?" Melinda hadn't mentioned any trouble. If she'd known, would she have allowed them to come? "What kind of trouble?"

"Nothing you need worry about. Just some people cutting across the ranch. Papa won't let the vigilante squad on the property to chase them."

Luis had said he was expecting someone to talk about horses. Christine's radar was alerted, but she would ask about it later. Right now, her only concern was Rebekah.

Roberto dropped her at the parking lot and gave her his phone number in case she needed a return pickup. A quick buggy trip put Christine at the quilt store.

She stepped into the cheerful room, but this time she didn't allow herself to get distracted by all the lovely merchandise. She scanned the room until she found Rebekah with an elderly couple examining baby quilts. The girl was being helpful enough, although Christine could see she was chafing to be done with them.

Rebekah excused herself and crossed to Christine. Her gaze darted around the crowded shop, and she sighed. "I can't leave right now. Can you stay until some of these families move on? It shouldn't be too long."

Christine agreed and wandered over to watch the women quilting at the frame.

Mrs. Byler came and stood beside her. "Come, please." She beckoned Christine to a pair of chairs near the back. They sat, and she spoke in a low voice so as not to attract notice. "Ranger Larsen and I barely had a chance to speak with Bishop Troyer last night when he got your call. I visited the bishop again this morning, and he agrees that this has gone beyond Samuel being missing. If a man has been killed, we must allow the Rangers to investigate. We will answer any questions, and we will pray for them of course."

"Thank you," Christine said. "I know this has been hard on you." She studied her hands clasped in her lap. "Would you mind if I asked a question?"

Mrs. Byler inclined her head, inviting Christine to speak.

"How do you reach this level of faith?" She took a deep breath and slowly let it out while the woman waited patiently. "I believe. I always thought my faith was strong. But you put me to shame."

Christine hung her head as she continued. "My mother was murdered many years ago. The reason I pursued my job was so I could bring men like those murderers to justice. I always thought it was a noble goal, but..." Her voice cracked, and she had to pause to clear her throat. "Someone asked me recently if I was seeking vengeance more than justice. I don't think I am, but it made me wonder if I've fully forgiven the men who killed my mother. I thought I had, but now I don't know."

Mrs. Byler wrapped her hands around Christine's clasped ones. "Do you think it is easy for us?" She shook her head. "If so, you are mistaken. The Lord preached forgiveness. It is what He wants from us. So we pray for the strength to offer it. We don't forgive on our own. We ask God's help. We ask that He help us forgive others as He forgives us." She squeezed Christine's hands. "I doubt my faith is any stronger than yours, but when you are raised in a culture like mine, it is easier I think, because you are surrounded by people who believe as you do, who support you in your faith."

Christine nodded. There was truth in that statement. She always felt more secure in her faith when she spent time in prayer and fellowship. She squeezed the woman's hands back. "Thank you. I will remember your advice."

"You are welcome. Ms. Davis, do not doubt the work you do. The Lord gave us each our special talents. I can see that He made you a fine lawyer. Use that for good.

"And now, my daughter is waiting to speak with you. She thinks I don't know, but I can see. She probably wishes to thank you herself."

The gracious woman rose and left Christine alone. She sent off a quick text to Blake telling him that the bishop had agreed to let the Rangers investigate, then followed as Rebekah beckoned her outside.

"I have to take you back to the workshop. I found something you need to see."

They headed down the street. Rebekah opened the front door and they stepped into the shop. It had clearly been put to rights after the incident last night. Even so, Christine was wary as she looked around.

Rebekah hurried to a desk and pulled a paper from the top drawer. "After you left last night, I remembered something, so I came back once it was light this morning." She handed Christine a letter.

Dearest Rebekah,

If you waited the ten days and are reading this, then something bad has happened. I know that sounds dramatic, but I'm scared I'll never see you again.

If you read this, and haven't seen me first, it probably means something happened to me, and Samuel is in danger. I want you to know I did everything I could to protect him. It's my fault he is in danger. It was my responsibility to protect him.

You taught me to read the Bible, and the Bible says "Greater love hath no man than this, that a man lay down his life for his friends." Samuel was my good friend, and your family welcomed me so kindly when I had no one. Because of my love for you, I love Samuel like a brother.

Please bring this letter to the sheriff. I know your family will prefer to pray and handle things on your own, but it will mean the difference between life and death to Samuel. Please do as I ask.

I will draw a map on the back with coordinates. That is where the sheriff will find Samuel. Yours, Johnny

Tremors shivered through Christine. "Rebekah, what does this mean?"

The girl was holding the edge of the paper, weeping softly. "It means my life is over."

Christine impulsively wrapped her arm around the young woman. "You know this man as more than your brother's friend?"

Rebekah nodded. "He was my love. Mammi did not approve of me seeing an *Englischer*, but he was studying with the bishop. He was to be baptized so we could marry.

"And now…and now…" She kneaded her hands in her lap. "The envelope said not to open for ten days after receipt. It had a heart on it. Silly girl that I am, I thought it was something romantic. I thought I wasn't supposed to open it because he had a surprise planned."

She sniffed and rubbed her eyes. "And all this time, he's been dead."

A fresh wave of tears followed her words, and Christine's heart broke.

"He's dead because he didn't cooperate. That's what happens to people who betray us." The harsh voice came from behind them.

Christine whirled around and froze. The man who had attacked them last night was standing with a rifle leveled at her heart. Panic clogged her throat. A million thoughts flashed through her head, but one drowned out them all. She'd promised Blake not to be stupid, and here she'd put both herself and Rebekah in danger. If anything happened to her now, he'd blame himself. But it was her fault. He'd been right. She was no better than Sofia, rushing into danger because she thought she knew better.

Calm settled over her. She cared too deeply to let Blake be burdened with her death. It wasn't his fault, yet he would blame himself for the rest of his life. Mrs. Troyer's words came back to her. *Ask for God's help.*

Lord, I have been foolish. Help me, guide me. Please show me Your way.

She turned to boldly face the man who was holding a gun on her. *The Lord is my shepherd.* She reached behind her back and brushed the letter from Rebekah's hands onto the floor. *I have nothing to fear.*

She'd been telling Blake she needed to protect herself. Here was her chance. She cleared her throat and faced him down. "You've been chasing me for a week. What do you want?"

He glared at her. "I want to know where Samuel is."

Christine didn't have to fake perplexity. "Why would you think I know? I never even met the man."

She saw a flicker of doubt in his eyes, and that strengthened her. "I ran into a building to get out of the storm. I know nothing about any of this."

He turned his gaze on Rebekah. "She does."

"I do," Rebekah agreed. "Take me and leave her alone."

In a flash, Christine saw that Rebekah was sacrificing herself. The grieving young woman thought she had nothing to live for. Christine couldn't let her make that foolish mistake.

The man's evil chuckle made her blood run cold. "Both of you, out the back door. I have Samuel's buggy hitched up. We'll take it to my truck." He prodded Rebekah with the tip of his rifle. "You drive." He shoved Christine ahead of him. "You're in the back with me. One wrong move from either of you, and you won't live to regret it."

EIGHTEEN

Blake glanced down as a message from Christine popped up on his phone. Bishop agreed to help.

Dread settled in his gut. How did she know that? He shot back a text. There was no reply. He followed it with another. Where are you?

He waited agonizing minutes, but there was still no reply. Glancing at the Rangers who were busy around the room working various angles of the case on computers and phones, he stood and headed for the door. "I'll be back."

He forced himself not to run across the kitchen, but when there was no sign of Christine in there or on the porch, he raced across the yard as Luis came out of the barn.

"Where is Christine? Have you seen her?"

"*Sí.* She went to New Grange."

Blake wanted to pull his hair out. "Why did she do that?"

"She got a call from one of the Amish and needed to go see her. I had Roberto take her."

Blake doubled over, resting his hands on his knees. She'd come in to tell him that, and he'd sent her away.

Breathe. This was doing her no good. He straightened. "Who is Roberto?"

"My son."

"Okay, okay. Where is he? I need to talk to him."

Luis pointed to the truck traveling along the drive. "That's him coming back now."

The truck pulled up, and a young man climbed down. Blake's heart sank and panic made his knees go weak. The foreman's son was the boy who had answered the phone when he'd called the number from the poster.

Blake charged toward the truck. "Where is she? What did you do with Christine?"

Roberto backed up, hands in the air. "Whoa, man. Chill. I dropped her off at New Grange like she asked."

"Then why isn't she answering her phone?"

The boy looked genuinely puzzled. "How would I know?"

Fear fueled Blake's temper. He throttled it back, took out his phone and scrolled through recent calls. "How about this?" He hit Call.

Roberto's phone rang. He yanked it from his pocket, and his face drained of color as he saw the number.

Luis stepped forward. "What's going on here?" he demanded.

Blake looked at Roberto. "No use running this time. Try talking."

Luis strode up to his son. "What is the meaning of this, *mi hijo*?"

"It's nothing to do with you." The youth sullenly picked at his hat. "I put up a poster because my friend went missing. This guy." He gestured at Blake with his thumb. "He called the number on the poster."

"And you ran," Blake challenged.

"Because you had questions not answers."

"I still have questions. What is your connection to Johnny?"

Roberto's head swung around. "How do you know his name?"

Blake turned to Luis. "How does he not know what is going on?"

"He wasn't home last night. Arrived back just after dawn."

"Where were you all night?"

"What business of it is yours?" Roberto's bravado was a little weaker this time.

Blake was done. "This ranch was attacked last night by the same men who killed your friend."

The remaining color blanched from Roberto's face. "Johnny's dead?"

"Has been for a week. So I'll ask again. Where were you last night?"

"Answer him, Roberto."

Roberto glanced from his father to Blake and back again. He tried for an air of defiance and couldn't quite manage it. "I was patrolling with my vigilante squad."

Luis exploded. "I told you to stay away from those people."

"You don't understand."

"No, *you* don't understand. They are bad people. They use young boys like you to cover their drug trafficking. They don't care about the ranches. They care about money."

Blake was quickly putting the pieces together, and he didn't have time to deal with an arrogant young vigilante. "They want Christine. She witnessed them murder Johnny."

"I don't believe you!"

"Frankly, I don't care what you believe. You're coming with me until I have her safe. Your only choice is whether I cuff you or not."

Luis turned to Blake. "He loves Christine like a big sister. He will come willingly, won't you, Roberto?"

The boy's bravado vanished, and he looked more like a scared teen. "I will."

Christine slowed her breathing and concentrated on listening, trying to figure out where she was. The last thing she remembered was fighting with the man in the back of the buggy and seeing a fist coming toward her head.

She focused on trying to keep her eyes shut. She had no idea where she was, what was happening or who else was here, and she didn't want to risk showing she was awake. She had to focus on what she could learn through her other senses. Concentrating on that should help keep terror at bay. *Lord, help me.*

Besides the sour odor of sweat, she could smell leather and dust. The dust made her nose twitch and threatened sneezes. Holding very still, she tried to take short, shallow breaths through her mouth and focus on what she could sense through her closed eyes.

It was still daytime. The room around her felt light. Other than that she couldn't tell much of anything. She could hear the man who had taken them, though. He was on the phone and didn't sound happy.

"No, she's still out cold."

Christine couldn't hear what was being said on the other end of the phone. She waited.

"I'll ask her when she wakes up." There was another long pause, before he spoke again. "What do you want me to do, pour cold water on her face?" Only his strange chuckle reassured Christine he wasn't serious.

"Maybe I'll put some dinner down next to her, see if the smell wakes her up."

Christine stifled her groan, but she was afraid there would be no way to keep her stomach from rumbling if he did that. In all her righteous anger, she'd again left without eating. Whatever he was cooking smelled spicy and delicious.

"Yeah, I'll get back to you."

She sensed him disconnect the call and felt the change in the air as he reentered the room. She waited, but he said nothing to anyone. That was a good sign he had no accomplices here, but where was Rebekah?

Approaching footsteps put her on notice, and she willed her body to relax.

She could feel him standing over her seconds before his boot nudged her hip. "Wake up. You need to talk."

Until she understood whether it was more in her interest to be in or out of consciousness, she had to stay still, so she focused on slow breaths.

He stomped away and a roar of anger accompanied the smell of something burning. That brought a small smile to her face. Knowing from the sounds that he was preoccupied with rescuing his burnt meal, she allowed herself to open her eyes a slit to take in her surroundings.

It looked like she was in a bunkhouse—one that hadn't been used by any proper cowboys in ages. Still, there were enough belongings scattered around to indicate the building was in use by more than one man. She fought back waves of pain and tried to concentrate.

This was obviously no working ranch. Out here, that meant the likely inhabitants were either drug traffickers or vigilantes. Although neither was a particularly good choice, it was starting to help the last week make sense.

Where was Rebekah? She slowly turned her head and gasped. Rebekah was tied to a chair in the corner. A gag prevented her from speaking, but her eyes were alert. And terrified as she looked past Christine.

"About time you woke up."

Christine's blood froze. She'd have kicked herself if her legs weren't already tied and she wasn't hurting so badly. She'd allowed herself to get distracted by the puzzle and forgotten to maintain the facade. Now she could only hope it hadn't been a fatal mistake.

She stared at him. "Who *are* you?"

He laughed. It was the scariest sound she'd heard since the gunshots nearly a week ago.

"I ask the questions around here. You give the answers."

NINETEEN

Every passing second felt like a lifetime as Blake summoned his backup, filled them in and divided them among trucks. "In case we have to go in more than one direction. Let's go. Roberto, Luis, you're with me." He wished he had his brother to help, but Dylan had been called out of town.

Blake started driving down the road he'd taken the previous day. Roberto stopped him. "There's a shortcut. It's how I took her before."

Blake debated trusting him, but a shortcut meant less time until he had Christine safe. He tried her phone once more as he drove, but there was still no response.

"Stop." Roberto tapped Blake on the shoulder. "That buggy wasn't there when I came this way before."

Blake didn't want to waste time on an abandoned buggy, but something about the way it was pulled off the road and ditched in a field of bluebonnets raised an alarm. He drove past, then pulled over. After alerting the Rangers in the other truck, he got out and cautiously approached.

The buggy looked fine, so why was it pulled off to the side of the road and left in a field of flowers with the horse still harnessed? "Hello, is anyone there? Do you need help?"

There was no reply, so Blake took a chance and hopped up to peer inside. The buggy was empty, though the inside looked like there had been a struggle. "There's no one here," he called. He was about to step down when a sunbeam glanced off something on the floor.

Blake knelt and thought he might be sick. Christine's bracelet lay on the floor.

"Wilson!" he called to one of the other Rangers. "We need a crime scene unit out here." He pointed at the bracelet. "Ms. Davis was wearing that when she left the ranch."

Blake studied the bracelet. His repair had held. The bracelet hadn't broken off in the struggle. Christine had deliberately taken it off. She'd left it as a clue for him. He bent his head against the side of the buggy as emotion swamped him. He'd told Christine he would protect her, and he'd failed when it mattered most.

Fear and anger surged through Blake as he rushed back to his truck and addressed Roberto and Luis. "Christine was in that buggy. She's gone now." He scrubbed his hands over his face. What to do? Maybe someone in the Amish village knew where they had gone. He looked at Roberto. "Do you have any idea where they'd take her?"

"I don't even know who took her."

To his credit, the kid looked petrified, so Blake believed him. "We'll have to go to New Grange and look for clues." He hopped in the truck and gunned the engine.

When they arrived in New Grange, Blake headed right to the restaurant. He needed Mrs. Byler, and at this time of day, that was most likely where she'd be.

Once he explained the situation, she hurried with him to the workshop. "One of the girls saw Rebekah driving the buggy away from the shop. She tried to call to her, but Rebekah ignored her."

Blake blew out a breath. "So we're looking for two missing women."

They entered the shop, and at first glance nothing seemed amiss. Frustration gnawed at Blake as he scanned the room. *Come on, Christine, what did you leave me?* If she'd left the bracelet for him to find in the buggy, surely she'd have left him something here, too.

He was about to concede there was nothing, when he spied a piece of paper peeking out from under the cabinet. He reached down and slid it out. "'Dearest Rebekah,'" he read.

"I think we've got a clue." He stepped out onto the porch and signaled to Roberto.

"Look at this." He handed him the letter.

Roberto's hands started to shake as he read. "I know what this is about." He looked up at Blake with terror in his eyes. "Samuel discovered that someone was using his furniture to carry drugs north." He shrugged. "I guess they figured no one would suspect the Amish. No disrespect meant, ma'am," he offered to a stunned Mrs. Byler. "Samuel wanted to confront them. Johnny was trying to talk him out of it, told him he was wrong." He bit down hard on his knuckle. "I'm guessing Johnny went in his place and they killed him. They must still be looking for Samuel."

A soft gasp reminded Blake that Samuel's mother was listening. He turned to her. "This letter tells me where to find your son. We will do our very best to bring him back to you."

She swallowed and nodded. "We will pray for your safety, and for Rebekah and Miss Davis."

Christine. Would she be there, too? Once they found Samuel, what reason did these men have to keep any of them alive?

He turned back to Roberto and Luis. "Do you know where this is?"

Both men nodded grimly. "It's on the Rivera ranch— where Johnny was raised," Luis answered.

Blake swallowed hard. Not what he wanted to hear, but it fit. The question was whether that was where they'd taken Christine. His gut said no. Knowing what they had done to Johnny, it was highly likely Christine had hidden that letter rather than let them see it. If that was the case, he needed to send people there to rescue Samuel, but where was Christine being held?

"Luis, the road where we found the buggy, is that on the way to the Rivera place?"

Luis understood immediately. "No, it's the opposite direction." He turned to Roberto. "Do you have any idea where they would have taken her?"

Roberto rubbed his eyes as he thought. "There's an old hunting cabin out that way. But they have warehouses and vigilante shacks all over the properties. They could have taken her to any of them."

Blake forced himself to think clearly, like he would if this was any other case and didn't involve a woman he was falling in love with. "Is there one in that direction that is more isolated than the others?"

Roberto nodded slowly. "Good thinking. There is one. It's pretty run-down, but it's where Willy and his brother lived when they were growing up."

Blake wished he had more solid information, but

every minute they wasted put Christine more at risk. "Let's start there. Luis, you know that one?" At the man's nod, he continued. "You stay with me so you can drive, and I'll coordinate as we go." Much as he wanted to keep Roberto within eyeshot, he didn't want to risk the boy endangering Christine if they ran into his vigilante squad. He would have Winston keep an eye on Roberto. "I'll send another pair of Rangers to rescue Samuel. Roberto, you go with them and show them the way."

Blake quickly brought the other Rangers up to speed, and they headed out in their various directions. If he could trust local law enforcement, he'd be sending far more backup into the field, but better to work with the men he knew and trusted.

Fifteen minutes of driving time after they passed the buggy put them a quarter mile from the house. Luis pulled over behind an abandoned barn. "We should go the rest of the way on foot so as not to give ourselves away. If we head that way through the fields, we should be able to stay out of the line of sight from the house."

Blake and Luis quickly made their way through the overgrown field until the ramshackle house came into sight. A barn and two outbuildings were in no better shape. The area directly around the house was cleared, but several stands of cottonwood trees and ground brush would provide cover as they crept closer.

"Look," Luis whispered. A thin strand of smoke could be seen coming from the chimney. Hope snuck into Blake's heart. The smoke, coupled with a truck parked outside, fueled it.

They flattened themselves in the grass, and Blake

studied the house through his binoculars. He could see a man pacing and maybe talking into a phone. The man came and stood by the window. Blake passed the binoculars to Luis. "Do you know him?"

Luis studied the man and nodded. "He's the Rivera foreman's brother, Frankie." Luis's face turned gray. "I met with his brother, Willy, this morning. He saw Roberto drive off with Christine and asked me where he was going. I told him Roberto was taking our guest to the Amish village. I didn't think anything of it because I've known Willy all my life." He hung his head. "Or thought I did. He texted a message and then left shortly after that. It's my fault they took Christine."

Hearing Luis blame himself chipped at Blake's own sense of guilt. Luis couldn't have known any more than he could. He slung an arm over Luis's shoulder. "We waste precious energy on guilt. Let's use it to rescue her, instead. Tell me what you know."

Luis looked skyward, and Blake had the sense he was uttering a prayer. Then he swallowed hard and spoke softly. "Frankie was the brother who couldn't measure up. The one who always got caught, always took the fall. But he worshipped Willy. He was away in prison for a few years. When he came back, he took a job on the Rivera ranch. It's all starting to make sense."

Blake took back the binoculars and studied Frankie. "So, he's not the guy in charge. We need to determine if there is anyone else inside. I'm calling for backup."

Blake kept a laser focus on the house as he dialed Winston's phone. Frustration built when there was no answer. He knew Christine must be terrified. After the work she'd done to fight her anxiety, to rebuild her confidence… It ate at him that all her progress could be undone because of greedy, corrupt men.

He wanted to storm the building and rescue her, but wisdom and training dictated there was too much he didn't know about the situation. "I'm going to circle around to the other side, see if I can see anything more."

"Don't move."

"What?" Blake turned his head to see Luis pointing a shotgun at him.

"Don't move. There's a rattler not a foot from you."

Blake slowly exhaled. For a moment he'd thought… "Can you get him?"

"I can shoot him, sure, but—"

Blake finished the thought. Frankie would hear them and know they were here. They'd lose the advantage of surprise. Of all the things to hinder their rescue, why did it have to be a snake?

The biblical symbolism hit him hard, and he raised his eyes to heaven. Christine had been praying and talking about her faith, and he'd ignored her. Maybe it took a snake to get his attention.

I shouldn't be trying to do this on my own, should I, Lord? He sighed softly. *I'm not good at trusting, more than a little rusty at praying. But I'll try.* He closed his eyes and concentrated. *Lord, help me to trust in You and have faith that You will keep Your daughter safe. Help her to find peace in You. Let her know that with Your help, I will rescue her.*

Please don't let her be afraid.

That last plea from his heart nearly broke him. *I'm coming, Christine. Don't be afraid.*

"Do you want me to shoot?"

Without moving, Blake glanced at his silent phone.

Going in without backup was unwise, but facing off
with a rattler wasn't any better. "I'm going to try to
ease back, instead. Keep him in your sights, and don't
shoot unless he starts to strike."

TWENTY

She had to stall.

From what she'd picked up eavesdropping, Christine knew they needed something from her. So long as she didn't give it to them, they'd keep her alive. She hoped. And each minute added more chance that Blake could find her.

Had he even noticed she was missing yet? Why hadn't she listened to him and stayed safely at the ranch?

She mentally shrugged off the guilt. This was not the time. She needed to stay alert and smart.

Her captor turned away from the window and strode toward her. "Where is he?"

"Who?"

He raised an arm as if to smack her, but Christine faced him defiantly. "I've told you repeatedly. I don't know anything. Apparently, I stumbled into something, but all I was trying to do was get out of the rain."

"Then why are you here?"

"Because you and your friends wouldn't leave me alone," she shot back. "What was I supposed to do, sit at home and wait for you to kill me?"

"Would have made everyone's lives a little easier."

"Not mine."

He actually laughed. "You're a bold one. Little good that it's going to do you." He kicked at her chair. "Talk."

Stall, Christine reminded herself. "You want me to talk, then you bring the Rivera brothers here. I want to talk to them."

His eyes widened. "They have nothing to do with what I need from you."

"But they have everything to do with what I need to know about their father murdering my mother."

Rebekah's gasp echoed his reaction. Christine just glared. "You can get back on your phone and tell them that's my final answer."

He grabbed his phone and stormed toward the front porch, leaving Christine and Rebekah alone. Christine quickly turned to Rebekah, who was staring at her with an expression somewhere between awe and fear. "We need to take advantage of his distraction. I know you sew, but how are you with knots?"

"I don't understand."

Christine explained. "He can't see you from where he is. Scoot your chair over behind me and see if you can undo the knots. If he wants to take us down, we're not going to make it easy on him."

Rebekah's face lit. "I have a talent for unknotting thread. Please the Lord this will be as easy." She inched her way across the floor, trying to make as little noise as possible.

"You're so brave the way you stand up to him."

Christine wished she could hug the girl. "I'm not so brave. I just pray for the courage to do what I have to. Right now that means doing whatever it takes to keep us alive until Blake gets here."

"You think he'll come?"

"I know he will."

Christine kept an eye on the door as Rebekah worked. The knots were tight, but the woman's deft fingers soon had Christine's hands swinging free. She shook them out to get the feeling back, then turned and untied Rebekah. "I'm going to tie them loosely back together so he doesn't suspect anything, but you'll be able to get free. We'll do the same with the ties around our ankles."

"Do you have a plan?"

Christine shrugged. "I'll be making that up as I go based on what he does. Stay alert and watch for my signals."

The phone conversation must not have been going well. Christine could hear her captor's voice rising.

"Then you come and talk to her yourself!"

Silence followed those words.

"Quick, back to where you were," Christine whispered. She put her hands back behind her back, and sat facing the door.

The man threw open the door and stomped his way to the kitchen, ignoring them as he passed, and stopping only long enough to set his gun and phone on the table. Christine was tempted to make a run for the weapon, but if she failed, she'd have lost the element of surprise. As she watched him bang pots and pans around, an idea took shape.

"What's your name?"

"So now you want to talk?" he snapped.

"Seems kind of rude to say, *Hey you, I'm hungry. I'm a pretty good cook. If you free me, I can fix something to make up for the meal you burned*."

He laughed that hoarse, slightly off-kilter laugh. "Nice try." He picked up the cast-iron skillet full of meat, eggs and potatoes and sauntered toward her.

"Hungry are you?" He lifted the pan to taunt her with the aroma. "Tell me what I need to know and—"

Christine swung her arms forward and used her palms to shove the skillet in his face as she launched herself out of the chair. He went down with a thud. She grabbed his gun off the table and held it on him as she waved Rebekah over. "Use those ropes to bind him." She smiled serenely at her captive. "She's good with knots."

Once she was done tying him, Rebekah grabbed a dish towel and shoved it in his mouth to gag him. Christine grinned despite the pain from the burns on her palms. "What a team—"

A single gunshot outside cut into their celebration. Terror filled Rebekah's eyes.

"It's too soon for the people he called to get here," Christine reassured her as she dashed to the window to check.

She stood to the side and scanned the front yard, then almost cried in relief when she saw Luis. He was signaling to someone around back. That someone had to be Blake.

Christine hurried to the back door and cautiously opened it a crack. When she saw Blake mounting the stairs, joy flooded her heart. She threw open the door and raced across the back porch. He barely had time to holster his gun before she launched into his arms.

His arms came around her as she clung to him. "You came," she whispered as she kissed his cheek. Blake turned his head ever so slightly so his lips met hers.

"I knew you would," she murmured before her lips settled into his kiss.

Blake wrapped his arms tightly around Christine as if he were holding on to life itself. Relief danced with a happiness he'd never known. He hadn't let her down. She was safe, and he was never letting her go. He kissed her gently, allowing the touch of his lips to share the emotion he couldn't yet find words to express.

When she finally drew back, she traced a finger along his jaw and a look of wonder filled her eyes.

"Christine," he murmured. A choked sob came from his left. He drew back slightly, still not letting Christine out of his arms. Rebekah stood in the doorway and the look on her face was one of such loneliness and heartbreak that it pierced his own joy.

"Oh, Rebekah."

He could tell from Christine's voice that she'd had the same reaction.

The interruption reminded him the danger wasn't done. "Where's Frankie? How did you get away?"

"That's his name?" She grinned. "He's tied up. Rebekah is awesome at knots."

She brought Blake inside to where Frankie lay hogtied on the floor. He could only shake his head in wonder. "That's one way to prove you can protect yourself," he teased Christine before stepping outside to confer with Luis about standing guard. He was taking no chances while he waited on backup.

His phone buzzed, and a smile burst across his face. He stepped back inside and turned to Rebekah. "It's my Ranger bud. They rescued your brother. He's good. Hungry some, and needing a bath, but grateful to be alive. They're taking him home now. I'll bring the rest of them here to pick up this guy."

"No." Christine cleared her throat. "I need to tell you something." She paused. "You're going to be mad."

He took a steadying breath and waited.

She gestured to Frankie. "He wanted to know where Samuel was. I wouldn't answer."

"Okay. It doesn't matter now."

"There's more." She dipped her head. "I needed to stall, so I told him to tell the Rivera brothers I would only speak to them."

Blake thought his head might explode. "Christine—" He took another deep breath and swallowed hard. He'd been about to remind her how dangerous a tactic that was and then caught himself. She was an adult woman, an assistant US attorney who had just freed herself and Rebekah from a kidnapper.

She eyed him. "Yes?"

"Nothing. Go on."

She gave him a secret smile that suggested she knew exactly what he'd been about to say. "I told him I would only talk to the Rivera brothers since their father killed my mother."

Blake's eyebrows shot up, but he held himself in check. *Water under the bridge.* "What did he say?"

"He relayed the message. And, if I overheard correctly, one or both of them are on the way." She inclined her head toward the man on the floor. "Frankie could tell you more."

Blake strode across the room and removed the gag. "What have you got to say to that? Your buddies are coming?"

Frankie said nothing.

Blake went to the door and called Luis in. They spoke quietly for a few moments before Luis approached the sullen young man. He shook his head sadly. "Frankie."

"You know him?" Christine asked.

"Since he was a boy." He turned back to Frankie. "I will tell you what I told my son. These men care nothing for you. They will turn on you as fast as they killed Johnny. You think she is the enemy?" He gestured to

Christine. "The drugs, they are the enemy. Money is the enemy. The men who use you are the enemy. Save yourself. Tell them what they need to know."

Frankie spit in his face.

Luis wiped his face in disgust, shrugged his shoulder and turned to Blake. "He's all yours."

Blake crossed his arms and let his gaze settle on Frankie. "Either way you're going back to jail. Right?" He looked over at Christine, who nodded her agreement.

"Probably for life."

Blake caught the first crack in Frankie's armor. "I would listen to her. Know who she is?"

"Some lawyer."

Blake laughed. "Try assistant US attorney. Or in other words, a very important and powerful lawyer." He walked toward the man. "And you tried to kill her. Multiple times. Kidnapping a federal official. Assault with intent to kill." He shook his head. "I'd be talking if I were in your boots." He shrugged, turned his back and took out his phone.

"Oh." He glanced over his shoulder. "You tried to kill me, too, so that makes it times two. And then there is the actual murder of Johnny."

"That wasn't me."

Blake walked back to him. "Now you have something to say?"

When there was no answer, Christine pulled Blake aside. "Don't waste your time on him. We need to set a plan in action before they get here."

"No. The only plan we need is getting you out of here before they arrive."

Chap aradu ol Piruse

Did arduci di di Blake. "Me were roming" Make wh
the facore. If this recon haoes oyaniage the Icoroy. Sive
yourself. I all usar, what they used to di ...."

TWENTY-ONE

"It's too late," Luis warned. "I see dust down the road.
Truck, car, can't tell, but somebody's coming."

Christine watched the anguish wash over Blake's
face before he could cover it, and something cracked
deep within her. She had been wrong to ask this of him.

She had selfishly focused on what she wanted and
refused to see what her demands were costing him.
Thoughts of him telling her about Sofia flooded her
brain. If she truly cared, she had to give him her trust.

"I'll take Rebekah out the back. We can hide in the
barn."

Blake glanced at her, his surprise visible on his face.

She reached for his hand. "You're right. I can't ask
you to risk people's lives." She gazed up at him solemnly, tears glimmering in her eyes. "I trust you to
arrest them. Do it for my mother."

Blake's eyes widened in visible relief. Christine
placed her palm on his cheek. "In case this doesn't end
the way we want, I need you to know it's not your fault.
Thank you for everything you've done for me." She rose
up on her toes, quickly kissed him and backed away.

He started to pull her back, but the sound of tires on

the drive stopped him. "Be safe," he called after her as she headed toward the door. She touched her fingers to her lips and sent him a kiss.

Christine led Rebekah through the back room, but as she got to the door, she heard the sound of a truck pulling up between the house and the barn. Too late.

"Blake," she called in an urgent whisper.

The look on his face told her he understood. They were trapped.

Christine heard slamming car doors. Blake took up position at the back door, Luis at the front.

"Rebekah, get behind the dresser." Christine dashed to the table where Frankie had left his gun. Blake glanced her way. "You know how to use that?"

"Of course."

He peered out the window. "That increases our odds, but stay down."

Panic threatened, but Christine forced it away. She had not come this far, fought this hard, to give in to a panic attack now. *Breathe. Calm down.* She took a deep breath, held it and released it slowly. *Please, Lord, guide me. And please protect Blake and Luis and Rebekah.*

Footsteps sounded on the porch. "Frankie. Open up."

Terror gripped Christine as she realized they'd left Frankie's gag off. She braced herself for him to call out a warning, but the only sound was a muffled groan. She looked back to see a triumphant Rebekah tying the knot in the gag. Relief made her sag against the chair leg. But there was no time for relief.

Blake held up a finger. *I have a plan,* he mouthed, as he pointed toward the open window. He ducked down below the windowsill and lifted his SIG, pointed it out the window and fired off a warning shot.

The bellow of rage came from Zeke. Ned's smooth voice followed. "Frankie, you've worked for my family a long time. I don't know what's going on in your head, but remember who pays you."

Blake let loose another round. Christine could hear the men retreat down the steps. She had no illusion they were leaving, but Blake's plan had bought them precious minutes. Hopefully, backup was on the way.

The sound of a rifle blast shattered the hope. The wooden door splintered as one of the brothers unleashed his rage.

Blake signaled to Luis to take up position by the other window and fire a shot. A howl of pain indicated he'd hit a target.

Christine crept up beside Blake. She could hear the men talking, but it wasn't possible to hear what they were saying until a voice rang out.

"Last chance, Frankie. Come out with the women now or we're burning you out."

Blake crouched down beside her. "You and Rebekah have to get out of here now. Go look out the front window. If there's no one out there, you can escape that way."

Agony tore through her. The idea of leaving him trapped in here... *Trust him*, she reminded herself. She nodded and scrambled across the room. Peering out the window, her heart sank. There was another truck pulling in, and she recognized the driver. It had been years since she had seen him, and he'd been much younger then, but there was no doubt this man was the foreman of the Rivera ranch.

He was talking on his phone, and when he got out

of the truck, he went to the back and pulled out a can of gasoline before heading around the back.

Christine gasped. He would do that? He would burn out his own brother?

"Blake! They're serious. Willy is bringing them a gallon of gasoline."

She watched him process the information and formulate a plan. He glanced at his phone. "Backup is five minutes out. We can't wait. Christine and Rebekah, I need you to stand by the door. Be ready to make a run for it as soon as the coast is clear. Luis, I need you to go with them. Get behind something that can shield you. The truck, a tree. Anything. Just get as far away as possible. I'm going to cause a distraction."

Terror brimmed over in Christine's heart. She knew that was code for *sacrifice myself to save you*. There had to be something she could do.

"Christine?"

She ran to him and threw her arms around him. "I love you. Please don't do this. There has to be another way."

His beautiful blue eyes shuttered. He was in full Ranger mode. "Go," he insisted. "Don't waste the chance."

Don't let my sacrifice be in vain. The words lay unspoken between them.

She gave his unyielding body a hard hug, then backed away. As she turned to leave, she spied Frankie's phone. Scooping it up, she ran for the front door, ready to wait for Blake's sign.

Blake pulled Frankie up and walked to the door. As he eased it open, he signaled to Christine to run. With Frankie in front of him, Blake opened the door. "I think you've made a mistake. Frankie hasn't turned on you.

In fact," Blake added, chuckling, "he's been rather disgustingly loyal."

Zeke's response was a bullet that embedded itself in the wall beside Blake's head.

"See, Frankie. That's how they reward loyalty." He shrugged and stepped back into the shelter of the doorway. He just needed to keep them talking until Christine, Rebekah and Luis got away. "I'm willing to consider a trade," he called out. "Our freedom for Frankie."

"Frankie, is Ms. Davis inside?" Ned called out.

Frankie nodded.

"Start pouring the gasoline, Willy." Ned's voice was terrifyingly cold.

Blake watched as Willy splashed the fuel and then tossed a match. He could only pray that Christine had followed directions and escaped. *Dear Lord, You who knows our need, please find her a way out. Please bring them to safety.*

Blake's phone buzzed. Backup was closing in, but that would do no good now. Flames were already licking at the porch.

He felt his phone vibrate again. Hopefully Winston would see the flames.

Ned's phone rang. Blake saw him glance down, then up at them.

"Hello? Who is this?"

Blake's heart sank. He knew who it was. There was a moment of silence, then the phone went on speaker.

"Obviously, I'm not Frankie. I'm using his phone, but I think I'm the one you really want."

"Ms. Davis."

"About time we meet face-to-face, don't you think? I'd like to make a deal."

"Christine, don't do this!" Blake shouted.

"I know you're planning to kill me, but I have something I want to say first—about my mother and your father. And justice."

Zeke snorted and pointed his rifle back at Blake, but Ned lifted his hand to stop him from shooting.

"Go on," he said into the phone.

"When this started, I had no idea who you were or that your father had my mother killed. It really was an accident that I witnessed Johnny's murder. But you couldn't let it go, let me go. So here we are. And I think it's past time justice was done."

There was a moment of silence before she continued. "Ranger Larsen didn't want me to confront you. He wanted me to stay safe." She paused, then proclaimed in a loud voice, "I'm no Sofia, Blake. I don't make useless gestures. I don't like them. Remember what you told me about support? How everybody needs backup sometimes. Everybody needs to rely on a friend, even a new one. We all need to have faith."

She was trying to tell him something, but Blake didn't understand. He could feel the heat of the flames now, and he knew he was out of time.

"Don't give up, Blake. Jump. Now!"

Suddenly a flash of gunfire erupted in the yard. Instinctively Blake pushed Frankie off the porch and jumped free of the inferno. A lasso sailed out from the barn, neatly settling over Zeke's shoulders. A bullet winged Ned just as another took Willy down. The Rangers had arrived.

They moved in, surrounding the three men. Blake grabbed Ned's phone. "Christine, where are you?"

Long moments passed without an answer, and then she walked around the corner of the smoldering cabin.

He'd never seen a sight so beautiful in all his life.

She ran to him, and he opened his arms to draw her in.

"That's the second time we escaped a fire," she whispered as he caught her close.

"Let's make sure it's the last."

He held her tight, afraid to believe she was actually safe. All around them Rangers worked cuffing their prisoners, reading their rights, but he couldn't surrender the woman in his arms. It was finally over. She was safe. "I love you, Christine," he murmured against her hair.

She pulled back. Her eyes were wide, but she lowered them. "You don't have to say that just because you were scared."

He tipped her chin up. "I was scared. But I don't love you because I was scared. I love you because of you." He held her close another minute. "You were incredible."

His voice shook and he needed a moment to gain control of his emotions. "This isn't the time or place for us to get into it, but I hope, once everything is resolved, we can have a discussion—about the future."

Christine smiled up at him. "I'll hold you to that."

TWENTY-TWO

A brilliant September sky belied the somber atmosphere as Christine and Blake made their way back from the cemetery to the Amish restaurant. Rebekah and her mother were waiting when they arrived.

"I'm glad the bishop gave his blessing for Johnny to be buried here, Rebekah," Christine said gently.

Rebekah smiled sadly. "*Ja*, it is comforting."

"The reason we came down today is that we have other news we hope you will find comforting," Blake added.

"Come in and sit a while," Mrs. Byler offered. "I will get you coffee and something to eat after your drive. Good news deserves pie, I think."

A grin split Blake's face. "I'll never say no to pie."

The restaurant wasn't crowded, so Mrs. Byler and Rebekah sat with them.

"Is Samuel here?" Christine asked. "I think he would like to hear this."

Christine noted how Mrs. Byler's face fell before she responded. "Samuel has gone north to visit family back in Indiana. But we will share your news with him."

"Will you tell them?" Christine asked Blake.

He smiled at her. "You deserve to be the one. Go ahead."

Christine hesitated. Now that the time was here, she wasn't quite sure how to broach the topic. She cleared her throat. "I know you believe in forgiveness. I admire that. But I hope you will take some satisfaction in justice, as well." She reached across the table to clasp Rebekah's hand. "I know nothing can bring Johnny back to you, but the case is now closed. The men who killed him will spend the rest of their lives behind bars."

Rebekah bowed her head in silence, and Christine felt the gentle squeeze of her hand. "Thank you," the girl whispered. "It will not stop me missing Johnny, but perhaps it will make things a little easier for Samuel."

"And for you?" Mrs. Byler asked Christine. "Does it mean you are now safe to live your life?"

Christine glanced at Blake, and a smile burst across her face. "It does. The Rivera brothers inspired no loyalty in the end. The men who worked for them came forward with evidence that ensures they will no longer be a threat to anyone."

Tears sparkled in Rebekah's eyes as she bravely lifted her face. "That is *gut*."

The chatted for a while longer, but the restaurant soon began to fill up for lunch, so Blake and Christine rose to say their goodbyes.

"Will you go for a drive with me?" Blake asked as they headed for the door.

Christine laughed. "Sure. All the way back to Austin since I have no other way to get home."

"I had a detour in mind."

Christine lifted her face to the sun. Life was *gut*, to

borrow Rebekah's word. "After all the detours we've shared, what's one more?"

Blake's shoulders shook as he held in a laugh.

"What? You find that funny?"

"Not really funny. Appropriate."

When Christine threw him a questioning look, he simply shook his head. "You'll have to wait and see."

They drove in companionable silence for a time, but as they drew closer to Austin, Christine felt the mood in the car shift. Tension built, rolling off Blake in waves. Finally she couldn't take it anymore.

"Blake, what's going on?"

He glanced over. "Sorry. I know I haven't been the best company. Bear with me, okay?"

When he looked at her like that, she had no defenses. "Of course."

She didn't question when he made the promised detour. Not long after that, as he drove down a winding road, she realized they were heading toward his ranch. She relaxed. Whatever it was that was stressing him couldn't be too bad if they were coming here.

Even after all the times she had been here in the past five months, Christine could only stare in rapt joy as they drove through the gates. Blake's ranch was everything her little-girl heart had ever yearned for.

Blake parked by the house. Christine got out of the car and leaned back to take in the stunning view. "You know, when Dylan told me you had a ranch in the Hill Country, I never expected this." She smiled over at him. "I feel so peaceful every time we come here." She shook her head. "I remember Dylan saying you rarely spent time at your ranch. Then you brought me here on our first real date, and I thought if this was mine, I'd never want to leave."

Blake's smile was like sun coming through the clouds. "I hoped you'd feel that way." He opened the trunk and removed a basket.

"Where did that come from?"

His eyes twinkled. "Patience, my love."

He took her hand and walked with her around the side of the house. Land stretched as far as the eye could see in every direction, but Christine's gaze, as always, was drawn to the fields where horses grazed.

Blake let out a long, exaggerated sigh. "I think I'll never be really sure if you love me or just my ranch."

Laughing, she spun around and into his arms. "No doubts allowed."

He smiled and kissed her lightly. "Walk with me?"

"Anywhere."

He led her along a path through the trees. "Dylan was right. Before you came into my life, I didn't spend much time here. But now, when I'm here with you, I never want to leave." He lifted her hand and kissed it. "I'm sorry I didn't have a chance to see you this week. Between tying up things with some cases and a few other things, it's been hectic."

"I understand."

"I just don't ever want you to think I'm too busy. I'll never be too busy for you."

Sensing his nerves, Christine raised a hand to his cheek. "I love you."

He covered her hand with his own. "I love you, too. And there's a part of me that's in awe that I'm even saying those words."

He sighed and stepped back. "All my life, I had such

strong opinions about my future and how there was no place in it for love or marriage. I let a child's view of my parents' failed marriage warp my feelings about love. I really believed, with every ounce of my soul, that the life of a family man was not for me."

He linked both her hands in his. "You changed that. You showed me that it's possible to work with someone and care for them, despite your fears and worries. That it's possible to have a true partnership. You made me believe I could have that, Christine. That we could."

Happy tears welled in her eyes.

"Last spring, when I thought I'd failed you, lost you? When I knew those men had you…" He stopped and she could see the emotion pouring off him, feel the tremble radiate down his arms.

He took a deep breath. "That kind of fear taught me that a true relationship needs God in it. I couldn't do it on my own. I couldn't find a way to cope on my own. When I tried to pray, I couldn't find the words. I was so scared. I was that little boy again, the one who watched his mother leave and waited and waited for her to come back."

He ducked his head. "My first reaction was to pull away. I couldn't do it again."

When he lifted his head, she could see joy replace the struggle in his eyes.

"That's when God intervened. He helped me see that if I walked away, I was losing you just as surely as if those men had taken you from me."

He wrapped his arms around her so her head was resting on his chest. "That loss would be worse because you weren't being taken, I was giving you away. I don't ever want to feel that way again."

Christine held him close. "You didn't give me away. And you can't chase me away. Blake, if I've learned anything these past five months and from our time with the Amish families, it's to stop trying to run the show. We have to let God lead the way, be open to what He might be trying to suggest in our lives."

Blake set the basket on the grass and stood before her. He gently brushed a wisp of hair from her face as his gaze held hers. His voice was gentle and hoarse when he finally spoke again. "What if it was meant to be? What if you ran out in front of my car that day because we were supposed to meet and fall in love, get married and raise a family together?"

Christine gave a nervous laugh. There was a depth and seriousness to his expression that she'd never seen before. It was amazing and terrifying to consider. "What are you saying, Blake?"

"I'm asking you to be part of my life, Christine."

He gently cupped her cheeks in his hands. "I love you so much." He paused slightly to give her time to breathe, then leaned in and kissed her.

"I love you, Christine. I love the way you changed my life by running in front of my car."

She drew back and took a breath. "I love you, too, Blake. I didn't think I would ever love someone. I had such plans, so much living to do." She shook her head. "You made me realize I was living for my mother, not for me.

"You saw through all of that. You saw what was driving me and what I had to fix. I was prepared to spend my whole life seeking the justice she'd been denied, and I didn't even realize that's what I was doing."

She blinked back tears. "But you helped me to see

that what I really needed was something to live for myself. I don't need to live my mother's dream. I need our dream."

Now it was her turn to lean in and kiss him. In his arms, she felt safe, cherished, all the things she'd thought would never be hers.

Blake eased back, and Christine watched in amusement as he bent down to open the basket. She was thinking of forever, and he was thinking of…food?

Blake lifted a quilt from the basket and shook it out before spreading it on the ground. As the beautiful handiwork was revealed, chills rippled through Christine. Something told her this had nothing to do with food after all.

"That's beautiful, Blake. Did you get it from Mrs. Byler?"

He nodded "It's a double wedding ring quilt, a gift of thanks from our Amish friends. They put it in the trunk while we were at the cemetery."

"You planned this?"

His eyes were dancing and he winked at her. "I've done a lot of planning this week."

He took her hand and helped her to sit on the quilt. Then he got down on his knee before her.

"I love you, Christine. So very much. I know we've only known each other for five months, but honestly, I knew after a week that I wanted to ask you this question."

He reached into his pocket and drew out a ring. "Will you marry me, Christine? Will you build a life and a family with me?"

Tears of joy flowed freely down her cheeks, so she could only nod and watch as he slipped the ring on her finger. As he kissed her there, on the beautifully crafted wedding ring quilt, she knew she was promising a lifetime.

When he finally pulled back, he was beaming. "You know that old saying about how the Lord works in mysterious ways?" He shook his head in amazement as she smiled. "That day you ran in front of my car, whoever would have believed?"

Christine smiled softly. "I guess it wasn't really the weatherman's fault. It was God's plan. We only had to open ourselves up to trust Him."

* * * * *

Dear Reader,

When I began this book, I had nothing more than a question. How would it feel to know you'd witnessed a crime, but no one believed you?

I had no idea where I was going with that until I had two serendipitous conversations, both of which centered around the Amish. As a result of those conversations, I started reading about the Amish, and became more and more intrigued. I live in NYC, and there are many days I yearn for the simplicity of Amish life. But more than that, I fell in love with the Amish for their sense of grace and forgiveness, for their giving up of self, and their absolute trust in God.

In my research, I also discovered the inspiring true account of how Amish youth from Indiana traveled to Texas to help out in the aftermath of Hurricane Ike. I asked myself, what if they stayed? If you'd like to learn more about this true event, check out a special section on my website at www.catenolanauthor.com.

You may not be ready to don a bonnet or give up your car any more than I am, but I hope in reading this book you grow in appreciation for a people who strive to live their lives close to the Lord, serving him all their days.

Blessings,
Cate

COMING NEXT MONTH FROM
Love Inspired Suspense

Available February 9, 2021

TRAILING A KILLER
K-9 Search and Rescue • by Carol J. Post

In the aftermath of a hurricane, Detective Erin Jeffries and her search-and-rescue dog discover Erin's ex, Cody Elbourne, buried in a building collapsed by explosives. Now Cody's the only one who can identify the man who set the charges that killed his grandfather...and the killer's dead set on hiding the truth.

AMISH COUNTRY SECRET
by Lenora Worth

After witnessing a murder ordered by her fiancé, Samantha Herndon seeks refuge in her Amish grandmother's empty home. But when she's caught in a tornado with criminals chasing her, her car winds up in Micah King's field. Can the Amish bachelor keep her alive...and convince her to stay?

IN NEED OF PROTECTION
by Jill Elizabeth Nelson

It's US deputy marshal Ethan Ridgeway's duty to protect a baby girl and her new guardian, Lara Werth, from someone who's determined to kidnap the infant. But as they flee from hired gunmen, shielding the pair who have captured his heart might be Ethan's hardest assignment yet.

UNDER SURVEILLANCE
by Jodie Bailey

When Macey Price survives a home invasion, she believes it's random. Undercover investigator Trey Blackburn knows otherwise. It must be tied to the suspicion that Macey's been selling military secrets—even if he believes she's innocent. With the attacks not stopping, it's up to Trey to save her.

HOSTAGE PURSUIT
Rock Solid Bounty Hunters • by Jenna Night

Just as bounty hunter Daisy Lopez is closing in on two bail-jumping mob hitmen, they kidnap her mother to force her to stop the hunt. But with help from her older brother's best friend, fellow bounty hunter Martin Silverdeer, can she rescue her mother...and foil the attempts on her own life?

VANISHED IN THE MOUNTAINS
by Tanya Stowe

Domestic violence counselor Dulcie Parker is determined to take down the human trafficking ring that she's discovered is working in the Four Corners area. And Deputy Sheriff Austin Turner is the only person she trusts to assist her. But can they expose the crime ring before she becomes the next victim?

LOOK FOR THESE AND OTHER LOVE INSPIRED BOOKS WHEREVER
BOOKS ARE SOLD, INCLUDING MOST BOOKSTORES, SUPERMARKETS,
DISCOUNT STORES AND DRUGSTORES.

LISCNM0121